Gifts from the Dark

A Miscellany of Dread

Compiled by Cake & Quill / Angelika Rust
Edited by Catherine Lenderi
Cover Design by Charlotte Stirling

First Edition October 2015

Copyright 2015 by Cake & Quill / Angelika Rust / Catherine Lenderi / Charlotte Stirling

For further information contact:
cakeandquill@fantasymail.de

All rights reserved. Any unauthorized reprint or use of this material is prohibited. No part of this book may be reproduced or transmitted in any form or by any means, electronic or mechanical, including photocopying, recording, or by any information storage and retrieval system without express written permission from the author/publisher.

All characters, places or events appearing in this work are entirely fictitious. Any resemblance to real persons, living or dead, is purely coincidental.

ISBN: 1518786529
ISBN-13: 978-1518786525

A word in advance

Once upon a time, there was a group of writers. They got along well, having much in common – their desire to hide away and write, their occasional need to crawl out of their holes and exchange thoughts and ideas, and their fondness for cake. One day, one of them – I admit, it was me – suggested they might as well team up and write something together. An anthology, to be precise. Agree on a theme, and go. Can't be so hard, can it? A theme was quickly decided upon. Make it dread, everybody said. Make it dark and creepy and anxiety-inducing. After all, we do love to give each other a good fright. And since writers are also people, with all the little fears, doubts, depressions and neuroses everyone carries, the question what to do with the money was just as quickly solved. Give it to a charity that works in the anxiety or mental disorder field. We finally found the perfect recipient in a small organization, which provides clinical support, as well as advocacy and other services, to mentally ill homeless in the LA area.

Before you start reading this, be aware. Some of the stories will creep you out, and some will make you laugh regardless. You'll meet stalkers and killers, aliens and demons, as every author approaches the theme from their peculiar point of view. There will also be blood and bad language, and UK as well as US spelling.

When you're done reading, please remember to leave a review, so we can hear your thoughts, and improve.

Angelika Rust, October 2015

Can You See Me

S.A. Shields

I can see her, but she can't see me.

My eyes follow her movements as she strolls along the pavement, sipping from a cardboard coffee cup. She looks sad today. Tired. But still perfect. Her brunette hair bounces on her shoulders as she walks. And the black pencil skirt that hugs her hips and arse. Oh, yes. She is beautiful.

But don't worry, my darling, soon I will save you from your dull, boring life. But not yet. Monday evening, you will see me. You will feel the connection. Yes. We are connected. We love each other.

You just don't know it yet.

***

Thank God it's five p.m. and Saturday is over. If someone had told me ten years ago that I would be a single, twenty-six year old working nine to five in a call centre, I would have laughed in their face. But here I am. Another day of angry customers yelling at me because their internet isn't working.

"I can't stand these evening shifts." Mia takes her headset off. "Has Darren thanked you for last night?"

I stretch my arms into my coat, then point to her computer screen. "You have calls to answer, you know?"

"They've only been on hold for a minute. They can wait. He's taking the mickey out of you, my love. When are you going to wake up and smell the coffee?"

She hasn't a clue what she's talking about. She may be twenty-two years my senior, but that doesn't mean she knows anything about my relationships. In fact, she's too old to know how relationships work these days.

"She's right."

I turn and spot Felix behind me, leaning against the wall. "Oh, stop your eavesdropping."

"He's constantly asking you to do his work," Mia adds. "What time were you up to last night?"

"He had a family matter last night. I offered to do his work."

She waves her hand. "Oh, it's always something with Darren. What was it last week? His dog was sick? Does he even have a dog?"

"Course he does." At least I think he does. "Anyway, he left a rose on my desk this morning. See." I hold the paper rose up to her. "He's not taking the mickey."

"How do you know that was from him? Anyone could've left it there."

I button my coat, grab my bag and chuck the rose in. "Goodnight, Mia." I shoot her a smile and join Felix. I've worked with him for five years, and he's about the only friend I can say I have. He's the only person I ever see out of work. I've never been so good with people. I prefer my own company.

"She is right, ya know? He's taking the piss out of you. Big time."

I groan under my breath as we head for the building's exit. "Why is everyone so interested in sticking their nose in my relationships?"

Felix laughs and holds his hands up. "Alright. I'll shut my gob. Just trying to help."

I don't want to talk about it. Because I know he's right. But I like Darren. I've had a crush on him for years, and if me filling in his call logs and responding to his client emails is the only way he will pay attention to me, then I'll do it.

I wrap my arms around my waist as we step outside. The icy air makes my face feel tight. I'm so sick of England and its crappy weather.

I reach my car. My pride and joy. My red Mini, which I'm still trying to pay off. "You coming back to mine for a brew?"

"Not tonight. Goin' out with a few mates."

"Are you staying in Manchester? Do you need a lift anywhere?"

"No, ta. I'm jumpin' on the bus. Why don't you come? Been asking you for ages to come out with us."

I smile and shake my head. I would much rather sit in my flat with a cup of tea, feeling sorry for myself while I wait for Darren to text me. Even though I know he won't.

Felix gives me a hug. "Suit yourself. See you back in the hell hole on Monday."

I watch him walk out of the car park. I often wonder if we would be a good match. We get on so well, but blond hair and blue eyes isn't my thing. And he's not tall enough. I'm probably not his type anyway. Besides, he has the name of a cat.

I get into my car and, with a sigh, dump my bag on the passenger seat. As I put the keys into the ignition, I do a double take. A rose. A paper rose on my dashboard.

I stare at it.

Did I take it out of my bag and put it there?

No, I didn't. I know I didn't.

I reach over to my bag. The paper rose that was left on my desk is still in there.

What on earth?

A shiver crawls down my spine as I look to my left, then my right, then behind me. Darren must have left another. But how did he get into my car? It was locked. I take the rose off the dashboard and throw it onto the back seat.

***

I hope you like the roses, my darling. I made them myself. Just for you. Don't be scared. They're tokens of my love for you; tokens to show you that wherever you go, I have been. Don't you understand? This is only the beginning. The beginning of our life together. I want to take you now. I can't help myself. Can't resist the urge to have you. To want you.

But no. Not yet. Monday evening is close.

Months of watching your every move cannot be ruined by my impatience. It needs to be perfect. It will be perfect. Don't worry. I will look after you. Care for you. Love you the way you deserve to be loved.

Why do you waste your time on that vile man, Darren? You deserve so much better. Even Felix isn't good enough for you, is he? But I will be.

Open your eyes, Angelika.

Can you see me?

***

It's just weird. I don't understand it at all. It makes no sense. My car was definitely locked. The more I think about it, the more it's starting to freak me out. Maybe it's just Mia, or Felix – their idea of a joke.

I pop my keys into the door of my flat.

"Is that you, Angelika?"

"Yes, Mrs Dobson, it's only me. Not to worry."

My seventy-eight year old neighbour opens her door.

"Hello, love. I'm sorry to trouble you after you've just arrived back…"

Here we go again. She needs some tea bags.

"Could you pop to the local store? I'm all out of tea bags and I'm parched."

"Course I can. I need to get some myself, actually. You go back inside. It's nippy in this hallway."

The man who lives in the flat above me comes through the communal entrance. I don't know him, even after a year of living in this place. I've never spoken to him past a greeting.

I give him a smile. "Evening."

He nods and smiles like he always does, before taking the steps upstairs. He always looks like he's in such a rush. I often wonder what could be so important that he needs to take the steps two at a time.

Out into the freezing air again. I walk along the pathway, teeth chattering and arms tight around my waist. At least Tesco is right next door. In and out of the shop in a flash, I stroll back toward my flat, the carrier bag rustling in the wind. My iPhone bleeps.

A number I don't recognise. I open the message.

Roses are red
Violets are blue
You can't see me
But I can see you

I stop walking and, as casually as I can, peer in all directions. This is stupid. I let out a laugh. Someone is playing jokes on me. First the roses. Now this. I text back.

Very funny Felix. Enjoy your night x

A reply comes through almost instantly.

My name isn't Felix.

Whatever. I'm not playing along with this stupid joke.
Once inside, I take the tea bags to Mrs Dobson, do her a cup of tea and make sure her heating is set properly on the timer. "I'll just be next door if you need anything else."
Finally. Home sweet home. Coat off. Shoes off. Kettle on, and leftover stir-fry in the microwave.
Who needs a social life when I can be lazy on my couch and get stuck into my romance novel? Nighty on, mug of tea in one hand and bowl of food in the other, I walk toward the sofa. Then I stop. The blood drains from my face.
Is…is that? No. What the fuck?
Slowly, I pop the bowl and mug down and take my novel off the coffee table. I close my eyes and open them again. I must be seeing things. But I'm not. It's there, in place of my book mark.
A paper rose.

***

How can this be real? This sort of thing only happens in movies. Not in reality. Not to me. Both officers have looked around my flat, but to no avail. Everything's secure. No sign of forced entry or tampering with the lock. Questioning my neighbours has also ended up useless. Mrs Dobson, and the woman upstairs don't recall hearing or seeing anyone, and the officers get no answer from the man's flat upstairs. I've spent the past five minutes being questioned by one of the officers.
The mug of tea shakes in my trembling hands. "No… there's no one. My parents died when I was a child and

my foster parents live in Somerset. But I have a great relationship with them. The only friends I have are work colleagues. And I'm positive no one from work has a grudge against me."

"And these paper roses, you said today is the first time they've appeared?"

"Yes."

"Do you have any past relationships that ended badly?"

"No, I've only ever had one serious boyfriend and that was a mutual ending."

"Thanks, Miss Cooney. I want you to be assured that you are safe. We've searched every inch of your flat and we have no reason to believe there's any foul play going on. Like you said, this is probably someone's idea of a sick joke." He gets to his feet and hands me a pamphlet. "In the meantime, we have your details, and if you believe you're in danger, don't hesitate to contact us again. There's some information in the leaflet about the crisis intervention team, support groups in the area and so on."

I have no idea what he's going on about. My brain won't take anything in. "Do you think I'm in danger?"

He gives me a small smile. "I have no reason to suspect you are in any immediate danger. But it's best to have measures and precautions in place. Before we go, is there anyone we can call for you? Friends or family?"

"No…I'll do that. But thank you."

Once I see the officers out, I sit on the couch and flip through the pamphlet. I didn't even look at it when he handed it to me. But the words on the front of the page make my stomach turn.

Stalking: What you need to know.

***

You've made me mad, Angelika. Can't you see I'm doing this because I love you? You should appreciate the roses. You should appreciate the time I've spent on you. What do you expect the police to do? They won't take you seriously, not until it's too late. They won't suspect how fast I move. They, like you, have no idea how long I've spent watching you. How long I've spent planning our escape. I'm not stupid. I haven't harassed you for months, leaving a trail for the police to sniff me out. No. I'm silent. I'm invisible. I don't exist.

God damn it, I love you. I'd do anything for you. I'd kill you to love you.

Monday, my darling. It's nearly time.

***

Monday afternoon. Lunch break. How I've managed to get through half a day's work is beyond me. I sit on my own, my brain on overdrive, my eyes scanning the few people in the staff room. It could be anyone. Someone in this room. Someone could be watching me right now.

Hands cover my eyes and I startle. "Jesus!" I drop my chicken sandwich on my knee and pull the hands off my face. "Darren, don't do that to me. You nearly gave me a heart attack."

He laughs and strolls to the counter, flicking the kettle on. "Coffee?"

"Please, a strong one."

"Tired?"

My sandwich is everywhere on my knee. Not even going to bother eating it now. I get to my feet and dump it into the bin. "Yes. I haven't been sleeping too well."

Darren grins. He looks cute today. I love the way his messy, brown hair falls in front of his face, like he's just rolled out of bed and not bothered to brush it. "So, what

I've been hearing is true? You've got a stalker?"

My eyes widen. Damn Mia and her big gob. I knew I shouldn't have told her. "I don't know. Just someone playing a joke more than likely."

He hands me the steaming mug. "Well, if it's any consolation, if I was going to pick anyone to stalk, it would be you, beautiful." He winks.

Great. My cheeks are burning. "Is it you?"

He laughs. "Afraid not."

"Oh, was everything okay with that family problem you had Friday night?"

"Yeah, cheers for that!" Then he's gone.

Is that all I get? Cheers for that! For staying at work an extra two hours to do his sodding job. My own fault. He's taking the piss out of me and I'm letting him.

***

Back to my desk. Headset on. Here we go. How many customers are going to yell at me today? Like it's my fault their services are down.

"I'm so fed up of this job," I mumble to myself.

Mia glances at me while she chats away on her headset. I answer my first call. "Hi, there. My name's Angelika, could I take your account number, please?...Thank you. How can I help you this afternoon?...Not a problem, I'll just pop you on hold while I transfer you to the bills and payment team."

I take a sip from my coffee. My chest feels tight. The noise of the call centre has never bothered me. But today, all the voices are putting me on edge. My eyes dart everywhere. Could it be him? Or him? Maybe even her? God, this is ridiculous. I do not have a stalker!

"Hi, there. My name's Angelika, could I take your account number please?"

Silence.

I mentally sigh. "Could I take your account number, please?"

"Can you see me?"

My heart drives out of my chest. I rip the headset of and jump from my chair. "It's him! It's him! Mia!"

"I'm sorry to interrupt you, could you just hold the line?" Mia looks at me. "Whatever is wrong with you, my love?"

I stare at the headset, my body shaking. I point to the computer, my eyes blinded. "It's him…the one who left the roses."

Mia reaches over to my headset and pops it on. "Hello, how can I help?...Hello?" She takes it off.

"Angelika, there's no one there, love."

"There was! He…he…it was him." I raise my hands to my forehead. "Who is it?" I shout. "Which one of you pricks is doing this? Because it's not funny anymore!"

Voices simmer. Every eye in the call centre is on me.

Mia stands and places her hand on my shoulder. "Calm down, Angelika. This isn't the time or the place-"

I knock her hand away. "He was there. It was him."

***

Why is this happening to me? Am I going crazy? Is this even happening?

I sit in the boss's office, watching through the glass as police inspect every computer in the call centre. There's even a specialist here. One who works with all this technology lark. I've brought the whole call centre to a standstill. I feel beyond stupid.

"Angelika?"

"Sorry, what?"

"I was suggesting that maybe you should take a few days off. Have you been feeling stressed of late?"

I glare at my boss. He's a fairly attractive man in his

late forties. His dark hair is thinning at the front. "Frank, please don't pull that card on me. I'm not imagining this. There was someone on that phone and it was not a customer." I pop my mug of coffee on the desk. "He asked me if I could see him. I had a similar text on Saturday night before I found the rose in my flat."

He waves his hand. "I'm not pulling any card on you, Angelika. I just think it would be appropriate, given the circumstances, to take a few days' break. If there really is someone-"

"No. I won't. I'm not pausing my life because some freak is getting pleasure out of trying to fuck it up-"

"Angelika-"

"And I'd rather be at work. At least I know there are people around me, Frank. I'm safer here than I am at home."

"If that's what you want to do, that's fine by me. I'm just letting you know I have no problem with it if you did want to take some time off. And if you ever need to talk, Angelika…about anything, you know where I am."

His sympathetic voice is driving me mad. He thinks I'm crazy. Just like everyone else in this place thinks I've lost it. Maybe I have. Maybe I'm so sad and lonely I've subconsciously created a stalker.

***

Why are you scared? Didn't you like the sound of my voice? Didn't you recognise it? Did you not feel the connection? Because I did. I felt it. Like a strike of lightning to my heart.

The time is close until you're finally mine. Until you realise how much you love me. The excitement pulses through every muscle in my body. Yes. Every muscle.

I want to touch you. Feel you. Hear you breathe. I want you sprawled out in front of me. I want to feel your insides.

Oh, my darling, I cannot contain my excitement for much longer.
But no. Wait. Not yet...not yet.
The clock is ticking.
I know you want to leave now. I know you can't wait for me much longer. But patience...soon I will save you.
When you're all alone.
I will take what's mine.

***

"So, what? The police aren't doing anything about it?"

I glance to Felix before looking back to the road. My hands are shaking. I grip the wheel tighter. "They didn't find anything at work. The number that called was untraceable. And of all the frickin' calls they record for staff training, that call wasn't one of them. I feel like I'm going crazy. How does this happen in the space of two days?"

"Try not to stress. Like you said, it's probably someone playing jokes on you. If you let this guy know you're scared, he's gonna play at it more, you know?"

I nod. Thank God for Felix. And Thank God he's free for a brew tonight.

He sighs. "So have they not like, I dunno, got a patrol car watching you or anything?"

"No. You see, this guy, whoever he is, hasn't actually hurt me physically. I've never seen him, he's never come close to me. At least not that I know of. So there's no need for me to be watched. They don't believe I'm in any immediate danger."

"Suppose they're right. They're the cops, they know what they're talking about, right?"

"I bloody hope so."

As I get closer to my flat, my tummy churns. I really don't want to go in there. I don't want to be near the place. I feel violated. Someone was in my flat. They must have been to have left the rose. The locks were changed over the weekend, but I still don't want to go in there. My own flat. It doesn't feel like mine anymore.

"You okay?"

"Yes. Sorry...I'm just freaking out about going into the flat. I haven't slept properly in two days. Last night I was waking up every five minutes with my heart racing, and every little noise scared me half to death. I don't know what's wrong with me. I've never been like this before."

"It'll be okay. Look, I'll stay with you tonight, if you want? I mean, I'll kip on the couch, obviously. But if it makes you feel safer."

"No...no, I don't want to be a burden."

He laughs. "You're not a burden. Honestly, it's no big deal to me."

I pull into my parking space, keeping the engine running. My heart explodes when I glance to the front window of my flat. "Holy shit." I put my hand to my chest. "The-the..." I trail off and try to catch my breath.

"What? What is it?"

"The light! The fucking light is on."

Felix looks toward the flat, then back at me. "You sure you didn't leave it on?"

"No. I didn't. I never turn that light on in the daytime." Tears erupt from my eyes.

Felix unbuckles his belt and holds me close to his chest. "It's okay. I'll phone the police for you."

I pull away from him and wipe my eyes. "No...what are they going to do? I can't keep ringing them like this. I mean...God, what if you're right? I did have it on last night when I went to bed because I was scared. Maybe I just forgot to turn it back off. I'm losing the plot, Felix.

I'm going crazy."

The entrance door to the flat opens. The man from upstairs walks out. Coat up to his neck. Head bowed.

Him. It's him. It must be. He smiles at me every day. He lives above me. Oh, my God. He could be watching me through a spy hole or something. Without another thought, I jump out of the car and pace toward him. "Hey! Hey!"

He stops walking and looks up.

"Is it you?"

He smiles. "Sorry?"

"You're sick, you know that. Fucking sick!"

"What?"

Felix comes behind me and tugs my arm. "Angelika, leave it out. Come on, get back in the car."

"Be expecting a call from the police!" I yell as Felix drags me back to the car.

I climb in, my body shaking. Felix jumps in. "What was all that about? You can't just go accusing people-"

"It has to be him. He lives above me. He-he...oh, I don't know."

"Look, call the police and let them know you suspect it's him. You shouldn't have done that. If it is him, you're letting him know it's getting to you."

"Can I come to your place? I don't want to go into that flat."

"Sure. But err, my parents might be home."

I let go of a small giggle and wipe my eyes.

"Dude, the market is shit...it's cheaper to live with them."

"It's fine. Really. I'd rather be anywhere right now than here."

***

You think you're safe with Felix. But you're not.

Open your eyes, Angelika. Look.
It's almost time.
And once I have you, I'm never letting go.

***

I make the call to the police. An officer will be trying to contact the man in the flat above me again tonight. I've let them know I'm staying with a friend. My mind is bucking wild. It must be him. I can't think of anyone else. The thought that he might have cameras installed, or spy holes to look at me, makes my skin crawl. I never want to go back into the flat. Not until it's been inspected thoroughly.

Felix directs me to his place. It's a good twenty-minute drive from where I live. Once inside, I glance around the large kitchen, which is twice the size of my flat. "Are your parents rich or something?"

He laughs and takes his black trench coat off. I give him a small smile. He's actually kind of cute. Maybe I could like him more than a friend.

"My dad's an architect. Mum's his PA….looks like they're not home, anyway."

"An architect? So how did you end up working in call centre?" I laugh under my breath.

He raises an eyebrow as he fills the kettle and flicks it on. "You cheeky sod."

I laugh louder. "I'm sorry. Can't help it."

"Go and make yourself comfy in the living room. I'll be with you in a minute."

My heels clank the wooden floor as I leave the kitchen. Wow. It's so fancy in here I'm scared to touch anything. I sit on the brown leather corner sofa and stare at the humongous TV. Jeez. Maybe I should hook up with Felix. I laugh to myself as I slip out of my coat and fold it beside me on the couch. I glance around at family photos on the walls. A huge canvas of a man and woman, and what I assume to be baby Felix, rests above the fireplace.

"Here ya' go." Felix passes me a mug of tea.

"Thanks, Felix. I mean, really, thank you for letting me stay. I feel like I can breathe a bit better now." I take a sip.

"Not a problem."

I eye the open fireplace. "I've always loved those fireplaces. They're beautiful."

"Really? I'm not keen on them. Too country-ish. Doesn't really match all the modern stuff in here. I wouldn't dare say that to my mum. She's a complete OCD freak. She'll tear the whole thing out if I tell her I don't like it."

I laugh. Then a bang startles me. "What was that?"

Felix frowns and pops his mug down. "I dunno....probably a car door slamming outside or something."

My muscles tremble as I try to catch my breath. This is beyond ridiculous. I take a huge gulp of my drink, even though it burns my tongue.

Felix places his hand on my knee. "Don't worry. I've got the alarm on. No one can get in here."

I nod. "I'm sorry. I feel terrible, ruining your night like this."

"Will you stop…you're not ruining my night. I was only gonna be sat here on my own anyway. Let's put a film on and just relax."

Relax. Sounds easy enough. I can relax. Like Felix said, the alarm is on. No one can get in here. I'm being stupid. No one's going to hurt me. The police didn't seem overly concerned. So why am I? I sink back into the couch, cradling my warm mug as Felix flicks through the movie channels on cable.

A rustling sound makes me freeze. "What was that?"

"What?"

I hear it again. "That! Did you hear it?" I knock the rest of my tea back as if it's a shot of vodka.

"I think you're hearing things." It happens again. Louder this time. "Okay…I heard that. Wait here, I'll go check it out."

I sit on the edge of the sofa and put my empty mug on the coffee table. "Felix, no," I whisper. "Don't leave me on my own."

He gets to his feet and laughs. "Calm down. It's probably the cat in the kitchen."

"You have a cat?" Despite my racing heart, I let go of a laugh. "What's its name?"

Felix bows his head before looking back to me and smiling. "You're a funny girl, you know that? Wait here, I'll be right back."

"Okay. Hurry."

"The cat's name is Felix," he shouts from the kitchen, and I burst with laughter. At least he's making the situation a little less nerve-racking. I twiddle my thumbs on my lap. The rustling sound has gone. In fact, I don't hear anything apart from the TV.

What's taking him so long?

Another bang. This time I leap off the couch, dread spilling through me, making my knees weak.

Oh, Shit. Shit, shit, shit! "Felix?"

Nothing.

"Felix, answer me!" I yell, my voice breaking as tears sting my eyes. The room sways in front of me and I put my hand to my head. Fucking hell. I need to calm down. I'm making myself ill. Okay. Breathe. I can do this. I'll just walk into the kitchen and Felix will be in there, fixing a bowl of food for his cat, or something.

"Felix?" I say again, taking a few steps toward the kitchen. My feet are tingling. Pins and needles attacking my body. I have visions of finding his body in a pool of blood, and a masked man waiting for me.

Oh shit. Oh God. I can't breathe. I feel sick.

I step into the kitchen. He's not in here. I put my hand back to my forehead. "Felix?" My voice echoes in my ears. "This isn't funny." I tread down the hallway. The front door is open, the cold air blowing inside.

Felix steps inside and I jump from my skin. "Jesus fucking Christ. Are you trying to kill me?"

He closes the door and laughs. "Sorry, was just checking outside. No one's around. Must have been the cat."

"This relaxing thing isn't working out too well for me." I put my hand back to my clammy forehead.

He taps the code into the alarm's keypad and laughs. "Ah, I know what can help you relax."

"What?"

"Come upstairs. My dad's got this kick-ass massage chair in his office." He takes my hand and leads me back down the hall, through the kitchen, then up some stairs. My head is floating. As we reach the top of the stairs, I slump against him.

He frowns. "You alright?"

I clear my throat. "Yes. Yes. I'm fine." Even though I'm not. I think my legs are going numb. But it's just my mind playing tricks on me. A panic attack. Maybe that's what it is.

"It's just in here."

"What is? Your red room of pain, Mr Grey?"

He laughs. "Please don't tell me you've read that crap."

"It's not crap. It's…" I trail off. What the hell? My voice sounds weird. It's echoing. "Actually, Felix…I-I don't feel very well. Maybe I should-" Before I can finish speaking, Felix swings the door open.

Pictures of me. Everywhere. All over the walls. I blink repeatedly. I can't focus. Can't make sense of anything. "W-what is this?"

"Do you like it?"

His voice changes. It's deeper. The same voice I heard on the phone.

It's Felix. Oh, God.

Heart banging in my mouth, I act on my instinct to run and dart to my left, but as soon as I do, my legs buckle and I fall forward, my knees meeting the carpet, followed by my chest.

"No point in running."

I just about manage to turn myself over onto my back. Every muscle below my waist is numb.

A blurry figure appears over me. I try to stay conscious. I can't move. I'm stuck to the floor. "W-what's...h-happening," I stutter, trying to keep my eyes open.

He laughs. "It's okay. I drugged your tea. But don't worry, it won't harm you. Just knock you out for a while. And when you wake, you'll be in our new home. With me. I have a place no one will find us. We can be together. Forever."

"F-Felix," I moan. My lips are tingling. Everything is fizzling out around me.

His laugh bounces through my ears. "I told you. My name isn't Felix. Felix doesn't exist."

Consciousness slips away from me.

Everything goes black.

The Price of Love
Chloe Hammond

I know now
That when you leave
You will take half
of me with you.
Not a nice, neat, sliced half.
Nor a limb, or organ,
Like my heart.

But half
of all of me.
The iris of each eye
So I cannot see a future.
The fingers of each hand
So I cannot reach out.

You will take half
Of each lung
So I cannot breathe.
And tear in two each chamber
Of my heart
So it cannot beat.

You will peel away
The top layer
Of my skin
So I burn

Like a chipped tooth
Or ripped nail.

That is the vow I took.

Vicious People

J.R.Biery

Alma Hicks sat at the breakfast table, reading the paper and waiting for Harmon to finish his food. After his stroke, he seemed ornerier than ever. It hadn't done that much damage, since he was already using the chair to get around, but it made it harder for him to speak his mind. Without the chance to start out with a little profanity, he usually just grunted. She could tell what he wanted from the sound. Soft grunt was 'oh well, what the hell do you expect?' Deeper grunts were his expression of contempt and exasperation. But a loud one meant 'Go to hell, bitch/bastard' and she ignored those. Really ticked him off. She laughed in satisfaction and Harmon rolled his eyes her way.

"Just reading this article. There are so many degenerates out there these days."

He dropped his fork so the end clattered against her good china plate and she didn't need a grunt to know what he meant by that. Forty-nine years of marriage taught you to read more than the sounds a man made.

"It says there was a home invasion in Knoxville. An old man was tortured and two of his fingers were cut off. He was found alive two days later when a neighbor knocked on the door to check on him. Said he was worried, since he hadn't noticed Mr. Grace walking his dog. It is expected he will live." Harmon gave a soft grunt and she looked until she found the caption under a picture. "Says Mr. Grace is ninety-two and has lived alone since his wife's death four years ago. Of course this picture is from before, but he looks like a nice man." She turned the paper around and waited until Harmon had his glasses on and looked.

Suddenly she felt Harmon bumping the table. Out of habit, she tried to voice what she thought he was thinking, in order to calm him down. "It doesn't say, but I wonder if he was taped to the chair all that time. He must have been pretty stubborn. They said he was badly beaten, then they cut off fingers. You know they probably did one, waited awhile before doing the other."

Harmon was shaking with rage. "Isn't that awful, that's only about thirty miles from here. They might as well have killed him. He'll probably get moved into a nursing home somewhere, won't be allowed to take his dog."

Harmon gave a really loud grunt and pointed at the paper.

"That's about all it says, no wait, it says he was forced to sign a dozen blank checks. Banks have been notified not to cash them." She was reading to empty space. Harmon had wheeled over to the front room closet. She could hear his heavy breathing as he locked the wheels of his chair and struggled to stand up. If she thought he would let her, she would have gone to assist him. She heard the broken, staccato sounds he made when he finally gave vent to his feelings. She bet those were a slew of hells, shits, and damn-its.

Slowly, she rose and walked out to the living room, although she had enough sense not to try to help him open the box holding his pistol. She remembered what he'd told the nurse before the last stroke scrambled his speech. "I might be eighty, not twenty, but I can still hold and aim my own pistol."

He had it all on his lap. When he almost turned over the chair backing too quickly, she bit her tongue to stay still. He looked directly at her and Alma nodded. While he unlocked the wheels of his chair, she cleared the little white stand he used to hold his book and television remotes. He set the box down, then shakily removed the lid to take out his pistol. Some people, some fool women, might have wanted to help at this point. But she knew Harmon had been a law officer long enough to figure out how to clean and load his gun, even if it took him all day. What else did he have to do these days?

It was a week later before a man in a suit knocked at the door. Alma walked over and stood with her hand on the chain, her feet blocking the door as she asked, "Who is it?"

"Ma'am, I'm Detective Brooks. My partner and I are here to check on the well-being of the elderly residents in the community. I don't know if you've heard or read anything about the recent break-ins. May we come in to talk with you and your husband?"

Alma leaned against the door, ready to close it, but the man moved his foot to block the door. "Will you show me your I.D.?" she asked.

He held his wallet open to display a gold-colored badge. Alma recognized it was a fake I.D. It had San Francisco written on the shield. Silently behind the door, she shook her head at her husband.

Harmon looked out the window. He saw a car without insignia or a blue light and shook his head at her.

"We're not dressed for company," Alma said, still not moving away from the door. "Give me a minute to slip back into my dress. I'll be right back."

While she stalled, Harmon handed her the phone and she typed in 9-1-1.

The man at the door became impatient, ramming it with his shoulder to break the chain and force the door open. Alma pretended to faint as the door slipped open.

The man grabbed at her and she stabbed him in the eye with the pen she had been using to work her crossword puzzle. As the second man rushed forward, Harmon raised his gun, bracing his elbow on the armrest of the wheelchair. Very deliberately, he fired through the now open door.

The old couple huddled by the phone, waiting for a real person to answer. The computer-recorded voice sounded loud as they listened to it give a time that they should remain on hold.

Neither of the men were dead. Even over the recording they could hear their ragged breathing and moans. While Alma tried talking over the recording, Harmon wheeled over to the first man, the one with the ball-point pen in his eye and grunted softly to his wife. Shuddering, Alma reached beneath to fumble in the man's pocket. She removed a roll of gray tape, a folded pocket-knife and finally fished out the identification. She held out the phony badge. Harmon fumbled in his pocket, took out his glasses. Alma looked away and sighed. After he finished, Harmon dropped the badge and leaned over. Carefully, hand shaking, he put the gun to the man's head and went through the same staccato bursts that worked for profanity these days.

The wounded man lying across the doorsill started swearing for real. "Are you crazy? You can't just shoot people. Boy, are you in trouble now. I'm going to sue you, you stupid old bastard."

The sound of the revolver's explosion was muffled by the first fake policeman's head. The man sprawled in the doorway was now pleading, screaming at them. "Damn, you old mother-f---er. You can't just shoot people."

Harmon grunted at Alma. She hung up the phone.

The wounded man was trying desperately to grab the doorknob above his head, swearing and screaming for help. Harmon slowly aimed and fired. This time the shot made a mess as it traveled through the man's head. In the distance, they heard a siren.

Waiting, Alma looked around at all the gore. "This will take a lot to clean up."

Harmon grunted softly.

"Do you reckon he's right? That we'll get in trouble for shooting them."

Harmon smiled for the first time since his stroke. It was a little crooked, but it made her smile too. This time the noise he made sounded like a laugh. She wondered if one of the men in the squad car would remember their old commander.

She leaned down and kissed him, crooked smile and all. Sure as hell, these dead scum wouldn't be torturing any more nice old people.

Cake & Quill

Boo

Charlotte Stirling

Backing off you howl at me that
I scare you like bats on the wing.
Like fox earth and dark woods
Like liquorice and tasty things.

Then you caught me dancing with Sister moon
And making trouble with wax.
Grinding bone with seedy pods
And marking my face with ash!

But if you asked - I might forget
I could hum or turn or flee.
Even fall at the arc of your bleeding heart
As the woman you need to see.

So what's it to be?

A definite plan.
An empty man.
A step towards the sea.

Indivisible, impossible and there's you and me.

Cake & Quill

The Last One

James Warren McAllister

I can hear it, moving around outside the cave. Why did I pick *this* cave to hide in? The opening is too big, it can get in!

I am pretty sure I am the last one. I have received no communications in over two weeks now. The creatures hunt us down and kill us. It is the end of everything.

It is moving again, the clatter of its metal suit echoes off the rock. I have so little left to fight with. My flamer is empty, and there is nothing near here I can reload it with. I have not eaten since…a long time.

Once we were a great culture. We had families, hopes, dreams, art, music, love. Then they came and spread like a cancer across the land, killing us off, one by one, planting their food everywhere. They pushed us further and further north, into climates too cold to sustain us. But we tried.

We wanted to live.

We fought back, as best we could. But we were not equipped to defeat them. Oh, we made them pay dearly for every one of us they killed. Very dearly. For a time, it looked like we had won a kind of truce. But we had not won anything.

And now, I am the last one.

Legend has it that in the remote past, we traveled the stars, marveling at the wonders and the vastness of all creation. Somehow we lost that, and all of us ended up here, on this little ball of rock, water and sand. We met the killers here. At first, they welcomed us. They called us angels from heaven. We taught them how to work metal, build with stone, and to govern justly.

And then, one day, they started killing us. Now, we are no more. I am the last one, of that I am certain.

It is moving again, creeping into the cave. I hear it grating on the rocks as it slinks through the cave. It wants but to kill me, it has declared as much, in a loud, boastful voice. And I am weary now. Very weary. I am old, and I would not see the next spring even in happier times. This savage in a metal suit will find me and kill me. But I will not exhaust life's last breath without a fight, feeble as it may be.

There, the noise, closer!

Death comes.

Oh, Creation, I do not wish to pass from thy warm embrace into that cold, dark, loneliness beyond! Why must we all be killed in such an inglorious, brutal manner? Death, have you no heart?

There! I see it now. Light glints off the brute's armor. I have managed to kill one before, but it cost me an arm. And my family. Those metal suits, they are too strong for our weapons.

Except for the flamer. That terrifies these terrors! They run from it, but only to return again to slaughter us.

It is closer. I am frightened. I think of Jorrelle, my mate, the beautiful Jorrelle. How her tears flowed when they found our home and they butchered our children! I cannot bare the thoughts of what those lives could have been. Jorrelle! My love. She died as much from a broken heart as from the blows of the savages. Jorrelle! Forgive me, for I have failed you.

Here! The battle joined, you worthless, immoral abomination!

Struck!

Pain!

Lash out, again! Again! I've landed a good blow.
Pain!
Pain upon pain upon pain piercing pain!
Darkness closing in…

The savage is talking. No, I don't wish to pass hearing those boisterous words!

Jorrelle! It boasts it has killed me, the last Dragon.
I am sorry, so sorry, Jorrelle…

Cake & Quill

Whispers Of Lavender
William Douglas Frank

He possesses the face of an angel, hair of snow, and
lavender eyes eternally hollow.
I speak of one and all.
He is known by countless names, but truth exists in
none.
The Elder!
A simple name, yet if you hear it upon a man's tongue,
I suggest you find courage and greet the final divide.
For this is a sign your creator has arrived!
He speaks in a voice that lulls many into his arms.
He whispers dreams that claim our lives will be more.
But do not be fooled!
He is every God! Lies cling to his shadow!
His heart conceals no love!
Your world beckons Death!
(Run, run, The Elder is coming!)
He rises from the void, wearing nothing but white.
His eyes speak to the lonely, saying everything is all
right.
But do not welcome hope! He speaks nothing but lies!
All he craves is strife's endless cry!
(Run, run, The Elder is coming!)
Burn your beliefs! None shall save you!
Embrace the soothing embrace of life's last lie.
The path is before us! Do not fall victim to your
children's pleas!
Silence their pain! End this game! Come on! Let's die!

(Run, run, The Elder is coming!)
(Run, run, The Elder is coming!)
Gods, they are all a lie!
There is only The Elder wearing white.

The Place of the Lost
Tina Rath

"I don't know why you want to go down there at all. No, it won't be cooler in there! There's nowhere cool in this ghastly place. It will be hot and dark and dry and smelly. I don't believe they ever sacrificed anyone there at all. Place of the Lost! They've told us about sacrifices in every single tourist trap we've visited. If they'd *all* sacrificed people at *all* these wells and caves and ziggurats there wouldn't have been anyone left to do the sacrificing. I thought they killed prisoners of war, but the guides keep talking about *virgins* – "*plenty girls – young, fat, make the god very happy,*" – the man at that last place was positively drooling. It's not healthy.

"Yes, of course the wretched man wants me to come. There's probably an entrance fee, on top of what we've already paid for the trip, plus he's afraid of losing an extra tip. Well, he'll just have to do without me.

"No, I *don't* want a drink. It won't be properly cold and it'll just make me feel worse. Yes, I am. I thought I was better, but I had another nasty bout after breakfast. No, I shouldn't have come. I wish I hadn't. At least the hotel has air-conditioning and the bathroom is cleaned regularly. Not *well* but regularly. I can't go until the coach driver comes back. Does anyone *know* where he's gone, by the way? If he's spent the whole afternoon in a bar we should have quite a lively trip back. No, we *can't* afford a taxi. The drivers charge what they like and they seem to think we're millionaires. Besides I don't want to be left alone with any of those men. In a car. I don't know the way back to the hotel! He could take me anywhere. At best he could fill the car with his friends and relations and drive them anywhere he likes at my expense and at the worst… I could end up in the jungle with my throat cut or, well, I suppose at my age, just with my throat cut. No, of course not. *You* go down into that horrible place with the others. The sooner you go the sooner you'll come back and then we can all go back. Or I hope we can. We aren't going to see another sacrificial site today are we? Good.

"No, it's got *nothing* to do with my "time of life". Don't be tedious.

"Well, go on then! Place of the Lost indeed! If you ask me it was a – what do they call it – some kind of polite archaeological name, but it really means outdoor lavatory. It smells as if it's been used for something like that quite recently. Well, I can smell it from *here.* No? Well you never do. Men never seem to notice smells like that. Some sort of natural protection…

"*No!* I'll be fine. I'll try to find some shade."

Good. He's gone. This heat is quite unbearable! The sweat is just running down my face. Like tears, but not nearly so refreshing. And there's no use trying to mop it up, the tissues just *disintegrate.* Ugh! Now I've got lumps of sodden paper all over my face. I must look as if bits of my skin are peeling off with hideous sunburn or some dreadful skin disease…I probably *will* have a skin disease soon. I'm sure I've picked up some kind of parasite. There's this horrible *feeling* as if something's crawling about under my skin…

"No, I *don't* want a llama – well, because it doesn't really look very *like* a llama, does it? Oh. They grow like that? The roots or the llamas? Oh, no, no, no please go away...NO..."

I shouldn't stay here, I suppose. I'm literally a sitting

target. I could stroll about and look as if I were sight-seeing. But it's much too hot. And my feet hurt. These sandals fitted me perfectly when I first put them on, and now the flesh is positively *boiling* up between the straps. You'd think with all this sweating…and the other problem…that I'd be losing weight. But I seem to be *bloating.* The tops of my thighs rub against each other when I walk…the skin is *raw*…*so* painful – and if I did walk the vendors could still follow me around. If I don't move they may forget about me. Ah, there's another coach arriving. Another lot of tourists may distract their attention.

"No, thank you, I'm fine. I'm waiting for my husband. He's sight-seeing. Yes, I know…so silly!…I tried to dab the sweat off my face, and the tissue just fell to pieces. No, I never thought of that. A cold flannel in a thermos flask with some ice-cubes, yes that would be very refreshing. No, I've never had hot flushes to that extent, but I suppose…cologne tissues? Thank you very much, that's very kind. Thank you… Are you here with *your* husband? Men do seem to like this kind of thing. Oh. Oh I *am* sorry…"

At last…she's wandered off. Cologne? It *feels* like acid. My face is on fire. I must look as if I've been *flayed*…I wish I hadn't thought of that. That terrible place where we went yesterday and that horrible story about the priest capering about in the bloody skin of a sacrificed girl…brrr! I'm surprised I didn't have nightmares. If I'd managed to sleep for more than a few minutes at a time I might have done. Perhaps if I close my eyes I could get a little snooze here – but not with that sun beating in my eyes. Even through sunglasses. Even through my closed eyelids…No…I can't sleep.

I wish I hadn't come on this holiday. I should have said no. Robert could have gone without me. He'd really have enjoyed himself then. They've got some dead bodies he could have gone to look at – ice-mummies or something equally horrible. Those photographs! They said the little girl looked so calm and spiritual until they found she had a fractured skull. And the little boys had been vomiting with altitude sickness...Or those dreadful caves where you can dive down and see the skeletons... Honestly you'd expect that sort of macabre interest in children, and teenagers, but most of them grow out of it...I *worry* about Robert sometimes...He hasn't needed me with him for...how long?...I don't want to think of that. Why couldn't we have gone to a nice beach holiday somewhere? We might actually have managed a conversation ...Oh, now the sweat's streaming down again, but it's *stinging* thanks to that woman's stupid cologne tissues. Where's she gone? Oh, climbing those interminable steps. Whatever made her wear those shorts at her age? Does she even think of how she looks from the rear? Still, she was *trying* to be kind I suppose. She probably thought I was some poor confused old lady...

"Oh yes, all right then, give me a bottle of cola. Oh. Haven't you got anything cooler than that? No, no, that's all right. I asked for it, I'll pay for it. There. Well, that's what they cost at the hotel."

Oh, what I'd give for a proper cup of tea with fresh milk...ideally drunk at my own kitchen table...

"Oh all right then, here you are. Thank you, yes, you can open it for me..."

Ugh, it's luke-warm. If it was properly chilled it would at least cover up the peculiar taste... I can't see any date on it...I wonder...

"No, nothing else...er...Nada...Niente..."

Really they just keep on until you do buy something and then all the rest descend on you when they see you taking out your purse. I can't drink this. I don't think it's cola at all. Oh dear. I think I might be sick. Those poor little boys...

"Hallo again. Yes, I'm still waiting. Men, eh! – Oh, no, I am sorry…I forgot. Oh, yes. I see. *Very* like a llama. Well, I suppose they do give the root formation a bit of help – they probably carve them…well, no, the legs – I suppose they *are* the legs – yes – they're not quite all the same length. But you could prop it against something…are you off now? No, I wish I was…no, sadly I can't. I really do have to wait for my husband. He wouldn't know where I'd gone…but thank you very much. Yes, I hope we do. Which hotel?…do you know I've forgotten? So silly. I should have written it down. In case…My husband calls it the *Cucaracha*…which isn't very nice of him, of course, and really it's quite clean. Well…yes…Good bye."

Oh dear, whatever made me keep talking about my husband to that *poor* woman? And where is he? I wonder if I missed seeing him come out of that – place, and he's gone up all those steps to look at the wall. Not, according to her that there was anything to look *at*, but I expect they used to throw human sacrifices off it…Is anyone up there now? I can't see, there's too much glare. It must be nearly sunset. Perhaps it will get a bit cooler. Where *is* Robert? What can be so interesting in that cave? Oh, another lot of tourists are coming out. He must be with *them* – there – oh thank heavens, that's him…isn't it? No. Oh, they all look the same in those stupid straw hats. What *can* be keeping him? Really, if he ever had a moment's consideration…he knows I'm not well. I wish I hadn't told him to go off like that. I wish…

Tonight we'll have a drink on the terrace just the two of us. And watch the fireflies or whatever they are. We don't have to talk, just sit beside each other…that's the last of the group, coming out of – that place. He *couldn't* have walked past without seeing me. Unless – that woman – she was standing in front of me, and she was quite wide enough to block his view…perhaps *he* went off and took the spare seat on her coach. If he was upset because I wouldn't go into the cave with him…but he wouldn't have done that, would he? If he has I'll never forgive him. That will be that as far as I'm concerned… I'll…

"No, I'm waiting for my husband. Yes…he went into that – cave place. Oh – ages ago. Yes, perhaps he did come out and I missed him … yes he could have gone up those steps…yes, yes, that could be…no. His jacket's the wrong colour. I wonder…could someone have a look in the cave…just in case? It looks as if it might be rather dark in there. He could have fallen, twisted his ankle. *I don't know*…yes, there was a guide…I don't know… they all look… no, I don't mean that. Oh. There's definitely no one left inside? There aren't any holes, or side passages or anything like that where someone might… no he's not especially elderly! Yes he could have called for help if…No. He must have come out and I missed him. He won't be long, I'm sure…"

Thank heavens they've gone. All I have to do is sit quietly and wait for Robert. There are people coming down the steps now. How many? One, two, three, four men. One of them will be Robert. I – won't look. I won't watch them. I'll just sit and watch the sun-set, and any moment now Robert will come up to me and ask if I'm ready to move off, and we'll get on the coach…Oh. There's no one there now. They must have all come down. No. No Robert. There's only one coach left…

"No, no, thank you. I must wait for my husband. I'm sure he wouldn't have gone to the coach without me. Well, I would have seen him go past. Well, the coach will have to wait, that's all! Sorry. I didn't mean to shout. Yes, I can see it's getting dark. What do you mean? How can there be only one seat left on the coach? Well someone from the other party must have got onto the wrong one that's all. I don't understand what you're saying.

"No! No! I can't go anywhere! I have to wait for my husband!

"Don't you understand? My husband…he went into that cave…I *must* wait…no, I don't think I've been behaving oddly…no, I had a perfectly normal conversation with that woman. Naturally I mentioned my husband…I *told* you I'm waiting for him, and naturally I'm anxious. Anyone would be … he *must* be here…

"I must wait! I must wait for Robert…

"I've lost him. I've lost my husband… in this place… the place of the lost…oh, why doesn't anyone understand, why can't anyone help me?

"I've got to wait for my husband! I've got to wait for him! I've got to wait…"

Cake & Quill

Trapped

Rubianne Wood

Hi, I'm Joe Stanley. Hey, come talk to me. I've got a joke for you. Oh, I know you came to talk to the staff and you don't want to see me. I know down deep that you are scared of the way I look, but I will tell you my joke. I had a horrible dream last night. I was eating a giant marshmallow and when I woke up this morning, my pillow was gone. Hehe. I knew you would like that one. It's a real humdinger. Got a kick out of it, didn't you? I have another. I have a lot of them. I have to, in order to cover up what I really feel. I have to stomp all of it down—the pain, the loneliness. Hey, buddy. Won't you talk to me for just a moment?

Little girl, you don't have to be afraid. This metal thing is just a chair. I love kids. When they aren't afraid, they laugh with me instead of at me. They don't pity me or hate me because of what I am. Their smiles are genuine and care-free. I remember feeling like that. I remember before. Before…when I had friends and family that cared and came around. Tomorrow is my brother's birthday, you know. He'll be fifty-two. I never forget. No, I never forget, though I've been forgotten. I got him a card right here. It's a real belly whopper. He'll laugh so hard. I can't wait to see him. He'll be coming to see me…oh, I know he won't really come. Down deep, I know, but if he did, he would give a deep belly laugh. He would, I know.

Hey, guy, come over and talk to me. My name is Joe.

What do you know? There are some things that I could tell you. Things that I wish I could say. There are things I'm afraid of. Like that nighttime person that comes. They put me to bed early and have people in my house. I lie in the dark and hear them. They think I'm stupid and don't know. They laugh and I smell the booze and the drugs. I'm too scared to say anything. It's my house, but it doesn't matter. They know I can't get up and they hit me if I yell out. Sometimes, I wet the bed and lie here, cold and miserable all night while they are laughing with their friends on the other side of the door. He punched me once. Right in the chest. I don't say anything no more. His name? I don't rightly remember. Names are hard for me. So many through the years. So many faces. It doesn't matter. In the morning, I don't remember much of what happened the night before. Just terrifying, vague memories that I can't put into words.

Look, my day staff is here. Oh, thank you, thank you so much! I get out of this cold, wet bed. Get a good hot shower. There's one nice girl. Her name has changed over the years, I think it's Grace, or Ashley. I'm never sure. Just that she's kind and fixes me nice meals. She laughs at my jokes and seems happy to see me—the only one who is ever happy to see me. For a few hours, I don't feel afraid. She asks me how my night was. I don't want to say. Instead, I tell her a joke to make her smile. I can see the sadness in her eyes and I know that she suspects. There is nothing she can do and there is no use talking about something neither of us can help.

Another long night and I cry to myself in my bed. Makes me feel stupid, like a baby. It's the weekend and I know, because I check the calendar every day. It's Friday and my nice girl, what is her name? Janice? She won't be back until Monday. Until then, it's the mean one. I can hear the party in the other room. His voice carries. I know he's drunk. He's loud. Louder than usual.

I know something is going to happen. I can feel it inside. I shriek in frustration because my stupid legs won't work. My brain doesn't think fast enough to help myself, either. I hear the door slam open.

"Hey, Joe. Thought you could join the party," he says. I pretend to be asleep. "Since you wet the bed anyway, you might as well have some." He pours beer all over me. I shiver as the cold wet liquid runs down my face. It burns my eyes. I try to stay quiet. I know it will be better if I do. I can hear his friends in the room, laughing. "Hey, Joe, what do ya know?" he says, sending gales of laughter through the others. He slaps me across the face and I can't hold back any longer. I fight back, but I can't do much, lying in my bed. He hits me over and over. There's an emergency pull string by my bed. Somehow, I get to it and pull it just before everything goes black.

It's Monday morning and I get to go home. I told the nurse my joke and had her cackling. The state lady came to get me. She wheeled me into the house. All new staff, she promised. I didn't have to be afraid, anymore. I didn't tell her that it didn't matter. I smiled and told her a joke. I knew in my heart that nothing would change. I've been through it over and over. There would be one that was kind, one that didn't care, and one mean one to take the place of the one who left. Their names changed and their faces, but it was always the same.

The Wrong Girl

Angelika Rust

"What do you mean, unnatural behavior? What is she doing?"

*****

I approach the doors. They part for me without me touching a handle or anything. They simply slide open, inviting me to come in, so that's what I do. It's all chrome and glass. I'm amazed the people inside don't wear sunglasses. It's brilliant. Sparkling.

I shield my eyes and focus on the people. They are all in a rush. Like in an ants' nest. I imagine being the child with the stick, poking at the anthill and causing all that uproar. Cruel. I'm not like that.

Well, maybe a little. I once doused an ant trail in eau de cologne, and set it aflame. Crispy, perfumed ants. I smile at the thought. That was cruel, I have to admit it.

I notice that the people are casting me irritated looks. I'm doing something wrong. I always do. Dad used to call me his little wrong girl. It hasn't got any better since his death. What is it this time? Oh, right, I'm smiling, and for no apparent reason. That's not the done thing.

I smile even brighter. And why not? Everybody should be smiling in a place like this. It's an airport, after all. This place should be brimming with excitement, with fascination. Humankind's old dream of flying, finally come true. We should all be standing there with our mouths open, staring at this proof of human ingenuity. Airplanes. I mean, wow. Tons of metal. Destined to drop. Instead they fly. But rather than being flabbergasted, we act as if it's nothing. And we complain about the delays. The service. The sandwiches.

I'm still standing at the doors. Too close. I'm constantly triggering the mechanism. Swoosh, swoosh, the doors keep sliding open. A security guard approaches me. I look at him as apologetic as I can, and move on.

*****

"She came in, then just stood there, blocking the doors, for five minutes at least, gaping and grinning. You call that natural?"

"It's not a regular sight, I'll grant you that. But I wouldn't go so far as to call it unnatural. It may simply have been her first time at an airport."

"Yeah, right. A middle-aged, female Caucasian. Dressed in jeans, T-Shirt and sneakers. Not a child, no stone age garb, no medieval tunic, not even a dirndl. Forgive me if I'm hard pressed to believe a person like that has never seen an airport."

"You may have a point. All right, give me a moment. I'll be right with you."

*****

I've reached the escalator. Tentatively, I put one foot forward. I'm wary of escalators. All those stories people tell to frighten their children so they won't play on the moving stairway. "Beware, it will suck your feet in. It will cut your soles off. It will bite your hands off." I shudder involuntarily. I always make a point of placing my feet firmly on one step, and jump over the part where the escalator emerges from and disappears into the ground.

I hop on and lean on the handrail. It's always just the tiniest bit faster than the stairs. I hang on and watch my body tilt. I wonder, how long must an escalator be until I get so bent forward I lie flat?

I hop off again and walk on, a spring in my step. Once I've started hopping, there's no stopping me. Hopping, stopping, what a rhyme. Slopping. Shopping. Dropping. Flopping. Mopping. Mopping, yes. There's a woman mopping up the floor. Shiny, shiny floor. Fake marble. It can't be real marble. That would be much too expensive. I walk around her, careful not to tread on the part she has already worked on. She smiles at me and shakes her head as if to tell me I need not bother. There will be other people along shortly. They won't give a damn, and walk right over the freshly polished tiles. Nasty, dirty footprints. I smile back at her. I don't know if she appreciates my effort or feels laughed at. I want to find out.

I sit myself down on a chair. Orange plastic. Smooth. Hard. I turn to the woman and watch. A man comes up the escalator I've just vacated. His gaze is fixed on some point before him. He doesn't even notice the cleaning woman. He wipes sweat from his brow and almost stumbles over her bucket. She stoops quickly to keep it from falling over and spilling its soapy contents. The man doesn't bother with an apology. He doesn't even realize the almost-accident. He only grabs his briefcase tighter and struts on with a purpose.

The woman straightens up again. Our eyes meet. She gives me a lop-sided smile, a half-shrug and a raised eyebrow. "See?" her look seems to say. She appears at ease with her lot. Admirable. I want to do something for her.

There's a bakery a few steps further on. I walk in, and buy a coffee-to-go and a chocolate roll. Outside again, I put a napkin on the ugly orange plastic seat and lay a table for the woman, with the coffee, the roll, two sugar cubes and creamer. I walk over to her and take the mop out of her hand. "You sit down. I do the mopping."

She casts me an incredulous glance. There's even a bit of fear in her eyes. Oh, yes, the innate fear of the lunatic. "I'm sane. Promise," I whisper, winking. I'm not sure I'm telling the truth. I've never been completely stable, and since Dad's death last week I've been feeling like I'm coming apart at the seams.

She shakes her head, but complies. She eats quickly. Hurried, eager bites. She downs the coffee in one gulp. She must be scalding her tongue in the process. Hasn't she read the warning? Caution. Contents may be hot.

She comes back for her mop. "You call that a break?" I scoff. "With whom were you competing?"

She snatches the mop out of my unresisting hands. "Thank you," she breathes. "The cameras, you know? Any break will be deducted off my pay."

My jaw drops. I wonder if I've harmed her rather than done her some good. She smiles again, a fond, worried smile. "Thank you," she repeats.

I nod and turn away. I follow the funny little arrows on the floor to the next hall. They give me some sort of direction, at least.

I wish I knew where I was going.

I feel her eyes on my back till I'm out of her sight.

*****

"You know, I don't necessarily agree with your assessment of her being a danger to people, or herself, but I do agree, she exhibits a certain amount of irregularity."

"So what do you propose we do?"

"Send a team down to follow her at a discreet distance. My opinion is, she's a harmless lunatic. I don't see where she could possibly be hiding any weapons or some such about her person. But who knows. If she meets up with someone, things might get interesting rather quickly, and I'd like the boys down there just in case."

*****

I hop, skip, hop on the little arrows all the way to departure. I like the way they force my feet to turn this way and that. I don't have to think about my destination, the arrows are doing that for me. I don't know how I've come here, or where I'm going. I woke up after Dad's funeral and just started walking. That's all I've been doing for the past few days. Wandering around. Aimlessly. I can't even remember where I've slept, or whether I've slept at all.

I don't see the man until I hop right into him. The same one as before, the one who almost tripped the bucket. He lets out a muffled growl. Animal. I must have spooked him. I hope he's not going to bite me.

"Sorry," I offer and don the most angelic smile I can manage.

He only shakes his head, rapidly, and backs away from me. I must be a real fright. Or maybe it's not me. I turn around, but there's no monster lurking behind me. Only a pair of lazy security guards.

"Sorry," I repeat, turning back to the man, but he's already several feet away. His smell still surrounds me. Sweaty, nervous smell. Maybe it was the security guards after all that had frightened him. Maybe he's got something to hide. Bad place to have something to hide,

an airport. So much security. Police. Dogs. Cameras. Customs. I like customs. I like to keep something metal in my pockets, just to hear the beep beep beep and watch the flurry of activity breaking out.

I could have that now. Just buy a ticket to anywhere. I don't have any obligations. Nothing to keep me here, no job to show up at, no cat to feed. And more than enough money, after Dad's death. More than I could ever hope to spend. That's the only thing I remember clearly from the past week. The lawyer telling me I won't have a worry ever again. Nobody, not the lawyer and certainly not me, had known just how much Dad had squirreled away for me. So that I'd be okay without him. His little girl, who at the age of thirty-five still brought home dead birds, hoping Dad could revive them. His little wrong girl.

I search my pockets and find my passport. I smile as I make my way to the counter.

"Where's the next plane headed for?" I ask the woman. She's a real sweetie. Short and elderly. Wrinkled skin and wrinkled mind.

She looks at me shrewdly. "You're too late for the Bahamas," she tells me. There's a twinkle in her eyes. She understands. She, too, wants to go. "Last call was a minute ago. Any luggage?"

My head swings from side to side. A pendulum of negation.

"Good, good. Let's see. Next one you could reach without stressing yourself much goes to Tripoli."

Tripoli. I taste the name on my tongue. Tripoli. It tastes sweet, like sunshine and honey, and crunchy, like sand. I like it.

"Come with me?" I ask.

She laughs. I can see she's tempted. But she's got reasons to stay. Responsibilities. People who care for her. People she cares for. "I would, lovey, in an instant.

But no."

"Next time, then," I decree.

She laughs some more. "Next time," she agrees. "You're a gem."

A bit of fiddling around with her computer, and she hands me my tickets. I look at them. They make me grin. Open return, is printed on top. I hadn't even known that was possible.

"Just call the local airport when you're ready to come back," she tells me. "They'll put you on the next available flight."

"Great," I respond. And just like that, I have a plan. A place to go. Finally, a ladder to help me out of the hole Dad's death has pushed me into.

I make straight for customs.

*****

"Carefully now, guys. I really can't guess what she's up to, but make sure she gets the entire procedure. Strip her down, search every pore. This is getting weird."

*****

I jump and almost bump into that man again. They're coming at me from all sides. The whole armada. He brushes me aside and moves away quickly. He doesn't want to be associated with me as they home in on me, corner me, pin me.

The man is waved through. He wipes his forehead with a kerchief and clutches his briefcase tighter.

They're friendly, but firm. I'm ushered into a little room. I don't know what it is they're looking for. I panic briefly. It was just my belt. I left it around my waist because I wanted to hear the beep beep beep. I want to yell at them, but as I open my mouth, nothing comes out.

Only a strangled grunt. I panic a bit more. What if I have another seizure? Not now, not now. I can't afford that. They'd never let me fly.

My breathing evens as most of them leave again. Two women remain. I don't like the looks on their faces, but there's nothing I can do other than close my eyes.

*****

"Nothing."
"Nothing?"
"Yeah. Nothing."
"Damn. Right. Give her our apologies and send her on."

*****

I hurry through the tunnel to the plane. It's running late, because of me. Because of creepy fingers in tight plastic gloves, probing in places they had no right to.

I don't feel too well. Maybe I should go home.

No. I've earned this now. A treat, just for me. A getaway. And maybe, I'll never use that return ticket.

The stewardess shoves me through first class. Further on, towards the back, where the rabble sits. Rabble like me. First class is crowded. My eyes meet that man again. He's going to Tripoli, too. He's still sweating, poor baby, even with the air conditioning on full blast.

I let my gaze sweep over the rest of the high and mighty. I could be sitting here. I have the money. I just don't care.

There's someone who looks familiar. I may have seen him before. On TV. Or in the papers. A politician or something. I remember now. Something about a treaty and some vague threats. He's the reason first class is so full. Half of the seats are blocked by his bodyguards. He should be traveling on a private jet, if he's that afraid for his life.

The stewardess leads me to a place in the very back of the plane. I sit, and look out of the window. We're already moving. Behind me on the emergency seat, the stewardess is buckling herself in. I must have missed her performance with the life jackets and oxygen masks. Pity. I lean forward to untie my laces. I want to take my shoes off and make myself comfortable. It's going to be a long flight.

The boom is so loud, my hands are off my laces and over my ears before I even register the noise. And the pressure. And the heat. And the sudden silence. I wince back up and look out of the window again. We've stopped. Something with the engine, I think. I unbuckle my seat belt, get up and make my way back down the aisle. It's so smoky in here, I can hardly see the warped seats and the blood and the twisted bodies and the blood and the ripped-off arms and heads and the blood and those empty, staring eyes and the blood.

All I see is a black hole where a sweaty man with a briefcase used to sit.

Cake & Quill

Mr Bark

Charlotte Stirling

At midnight's eve when all is black
Make sure the door is at your back.
This is the time of all things dark
Bad things abroad like Mr Bark.

He likes a child or two for tea
And gathers them up by terrified three
His hat gleams bright with tears of fright
As he carries them off into the night.

For years bad children have been told
To behave or else they will be sold
To Mr Bark on a pitch, black day
For gold and silver so they say.

He stuffs them in rough sacks of teal
And loads them on a sledge of eels
That slither and slider all around
From journey's start to edge of town.

A child that escapes old Mr Bark
Will forever carry his fiendish mark
And always fear the smell of night

And lose their voice and half their height.

So if you want to outwit the Bark
Behave and listen to your heart
Respectful be of Mum and Dad
And safe you'll be and very glad.

Keep eyes closed tight when shadows creep
Towards the bed with claws and teeth.
Don't make a sound or look beneath
Your bed or in the wardrobe deep.

And Mr Bark might glide on by
and steal another for his childer pie.
And leave you dreaming in your sleep
Not running scared on the darkened Heath.

Phantom Dollhouse

William Douglas Frank

Dripping blood over a phantom dollhouse,
I whisper sour songs of an eternity long since past.
Oh, princess who has become pain,
how we danced amidst cruel screams in those dead
bright days.

Yet, now I wander an empty world and dip my nose in
the snow.
Where did our dreams go?
Oh, my rotted darling, can you hear the stream cease to
flow?
I hear it perfectly. I smirk at this thought.
I suffer for the pleasure.
This sickness won't fade.
An unfading echo....

Oh, Eliza! Look at me!
I am laughing, I am fading, I am breaking, I am
breathing!
What must I do to find meaning?
Lies, lies, lies, lies...
That is all they ask me to seek!
What is the purpose of our labor?
Where is the value in your week?
To Hell with this game!
My soul has begun to reek.

Lust, take me home.
Keep me confined!
Sever the line!
Shatter sorrow!
Envelop the world...
Protect me from time.

Love, fight my shadow!
You are ever so warm...
Don't leave me to battle the world's sickness alone.
I can feel your touch fading.
Have you finally gone home?

Sadism, rip a hole!
Slather some brains on the floor.
Burn a den of raptors to the ground!
Bring some harlot to her knees!
Corrode the souls of those who once ran free!

Humanity, stitch me up!
These obsessions are my own.
These sick games are my will.
These warring emotions will see me broken.
Oh, little sister, where did you go?

Night Bus

Russell Cruse

1

A call centre: I knew I'd end up in a call centre. And because I'm new, I get put on the swing shift – 5:00pm to 1:00 am. You'd think I'd be a bit pissed off that all an MPhil gets you these days is a job answering phones but, you see, my Master's thesis was on "Stoicism in Austerity Britain" and so as the Americans say, I "*suck it up*": a disturbingly accurate three word precis of the tenets of the Stoics. Seneca had it easy; a couple of hours of watching his lifeblood seep out into a warm bath. Me? Condemned to a slow death by taxation query.

But now I'm heading home: I've popped into the all-night supermarket and picked up, as usual, the first edition of tomorrow's... today's paper and now I'm at the bus-stop, waiting for the 109. Standing alone in a deserted street at one in the morning, it's always nice to see it drag its little pool of warm light around the corner of Paternoster Street and deliver it to where I stand.

I'd been surprised when I saw the state of the Night Bus the first time it ground its wheels against the pavement where I stood; I'd not expected it to be amongst the latest vehicles in the fleet; but an old B15? A Leyland Titan? Practically a museum piece with its "W" reg - in old money!

The wailing, mechanical complaints as it struggles to a standstill echo off the steel and glass canyon walls and with a thud and a hiss, rubber-edged doors usher me in.

It's always the same driver. I make a point of not simply waving my card over the reader and drifting past as others must do, but of wishing him a cheery, "Good Morning!" He has long stopped favouring me with even the desultory stare that used to serve as acknowledgement and he now merely twitches the lever that conjures up the hiss, rattle and clunk and seals me in.

A brief, unreturned smile to the woman in the headscarf and a quick glance at the LD before I go upstairs.

LD? Oh, that's just what I call the group that occupies – and it does occupy – much of the Lower Deck of the 109. Animated and talkative, its conversations punctuated by gales of laughter, it actually lifted my spirits when I first encountered it. No longer.

At first I'd sit with the LD, hoping to at least make an acquaintance or two but it wasn't to be. Barely three stops after I get on, the entire LD gets off. For a while, I would sit there alone, but without the hubbub of voices, the clatter and crash of the ancient engine just a couple of feet and an aluminium bulkhead away, combined with a strong stink of inefficiently burned diesel soon drove me upstairs.

Now, from my perch, as the 109 pulls into London Bridge, I observe the LD being excreted en masse to separate and gush into that vast concatenation of culverts and tunnels draining into the suburbs of South London.

After just two more stops, the woman disembarks. I smear a small arc in the condensation and peer down upon her blue and white spotted headscarf and witness her nightly struggle to extend the handle of a tartan shopping trolley. The driver steers away her only light long before her task is complete and I wonder why she doesn't get it fixed; or get a new trolley; or at least get the handle out before she gets off. Time was, on the old Routemasters, a conductor might have done it for her for nothing but a thank you and a smile and would have seen her safely on her way before pressing the little red button to ding the driver into action.

No doubt, the miserable bugger in charge of the 109 just sits and watches and as soon as she clears the platform, it's hiss, rattle, clunk and away.

Then it's just me and the young couple.

Usually.

I assume they're a couple because they sit next to each other, three rows from the back and four behind me. I thought at first that the odour was the legacy of years of top-deck smoking, but I'll swear it's getting worse. I reckon the pair of them have a crafty fag before anyone gets on. I seldom hear them speak and even now they rise, wordlessly, from their seats. The smell of stale cigarette smoke increases as they approach and in the bulbous fish-eye above the stairwell, I watch their unsteady progress down the central aisle, jerking from seat-back to seat-back like two sailors in a squall until first he then she disappears through the hatchway that leads, appropriately, to the lower deck.

The bus stops a third time and the young couple are disgorged onto the pavement. He, hands thrust into the side pockets of a tightly-zipped leather jacket, hunches his shoulders and strides away; she clatters along behind, three steps to his two, swaddled as she is in tight leggings and fur-trimmed jacket.

Now, alone, the recognisable and familiar events of my journey over, there is nothing to do but allow myself to be conveyed through the ever-darkening streets towards my own destination.

And so it goes for the first several weeks; so it goes until a few nights back; when the bulb went out.

Well, I say, "bulb" – more like a little striplight,

really. Anyway, it's the one at the back of the right hand row; I notice it out of the corner of my eye; a shimmer, followed by a gentle tinkling sound and it's gone. I turn to look and sure enough, I see a long, dull rectangle in a grey-black puddle of dark and in the rear right hand seat, something else.

You always think it's your eyes playing tricks and usually it is and that's what I think at first, but I'm wrong. There is someone there. It's dim at the back now and I'm able to see little more than a huddled outline, but it's definitely a person; a passenger. I smile, as one does, jerk my head in the direction of the blown light. I don't know why; I suppose it's the desire to be recognised as a fellow player in a tiny drama. I never expect a response from any denizen of the 109 and I'm not disappointed now. Turning back, I settle into my seat. Bloody old bus; stinks of diesel and smoke and it tries to knock my teeth out as it jumps, jogs and clatters on through the night.

I have fallen asleep a couple of times on the bus and I don't like it much, so I try to keep awake, but some nights… Anyway, I feel myself beginning to nod off. I'm aware that I've relaxed my grip on the paper and it's resting in my lap.

In my dream, the top deck is full of young couples smoking and I'm choking, unable to breathe. I can't get them, however much I try, to put out their cigarettes and I start to cough – for real. Opening my eyes, I realise immediately that I've been dreaming; however, the coughing continues. There is smoke and (God!) there is flame. I leap up and the paper, now well alight falls to the floor. I stamp on it, sending charred and glowing remnants twirling into the darkness at the rear of the bus.

People do it; I mean, I've seen it done when I was student: setting people's newspapers on fire. It can be a laugh; in the park; with your mates. But not on a bus and not to total strangers! Livid, I turn around. And he's not there; I mean he's gone – got off. He must have set light to my paper as he walked past. Tosser! Knowing my luck, he'll have filmed it and it'll be on the net before I get home.

On the bright side, it did wake me up and the Stoic in me muses on this as I walk the hundred metres from my stop to my bedsit.

2

By next evening, the anxieties of tax claimants have driven all thoughts of the previous night's events from my mind even as I climb onto the top deck of the 109 and even as the smell of old smoke assails my nostrils. The young couple is there, third seat from the back as usual, but behind them and to their right, I notice that the bulb is out. Still. Neither of the couple glances in my direction as I take my usual seat and we bounce along until the murmur punctuated by mirth that is the LD alights at London Bridge.

My thoughts trundle along unimpeded until they, with the bus, come to a halt when the woman gets off. Her spotted headscarf bobs up and down in time with her tugs on the recalcitrant handle of her trolley until, only seconds later, she drifts behind and beneath me into the darkness, like someone drowning.

tinkle

I look up and notice that a subtle change has taken place. Glancing at the fish-eye, I see the distorted reflection of the young couple half-turned in its double-seat inspecting the light that has just gone out.

They are speaking so quietly that I cannot hear. I catch the word, "shit" and the phrase, "…wiring loom's fucked…" but that's all. And now the entire back of the bus, rear lamps, left and right extinguished, is in darkness. It's surprising, the effect of the loss of just two lights. And now the young couple stand, stagger and descend. A whiff of stale cigs and they are gone.

And then a thought; a stupid, irrational, unworthy thought. My hind-brain generates it and when it finally seeps into my consciousness, there is no way I can avoid turning my head. I do it slowly until I ask myself why I feel the need to. When I see that the rear right-side seat is indeed vacant, I let my lungs empty before even realising that I'd not been breathing.

But.

With the city way behind and suburbia approaching, the constant glare of shop windows and fluorescent lights has diminished and I notice how dark the loss of the lamps has made the top deck. The effect is heightened, if anything, when every five or ten seconds the sodium glow of a street-lamp runs through the 109 from front to back.

I'm just about to face forwards once more when something catches my eye.

The wash of light flows down the bus and on the wall, in the darkness by the rear seat, a shadow. It's cast – it has to be- by a figure; a hunched figure that must be seated on the opposite side of the bus, in the rear seat at the back of my row.

The mirror.

Three street-lamps drift by before I dare look. As a fourth approaches, I take a breath and force my eyes upward. There's no doubt: the passenger is there. For a moment, I'm nonplussed, but then I realise he could only have been hiding behind the seat, waiting until the young couple left before making his presence known. He's messing with me. And as the sodium glare, which can have lasted only a fraction of a second, sweeps over the figure, I catch three distinct reflections: two are clearly eyes, shining yellow and the third, a series of small spots blending into a serrated line.

Teeth.

Is he smiling at my discomfiture? Is he deliberately trying to unsettle me after what he did the night before? Is he the one who's been putting out the lamps? He could have done it easily. What's his game? Perhaps it's not just a bit of twisted fun. Perhaps he means to mug me.

Well, good luck. I've got precisely seven quid and an Oyster card.

But if he wanted to mug me, he'd have done it long before now. I think he's just bored and a bit pissed and having a laugh. Perhaps if I speak to him, he'll see that it hasn't worked and that I'm not to be bothered by his buggering about. I shan't threaten and I won't mention the broken lights to him (I might tell the driver when I get off, though. Tell him what? There are two lights out upstairs and I think the bloke on the back seat might have something to do with it?)

Don't think so.

I'm still weighing the pros and cons of speaking to him when I realise that my stop is coming up. O.K. No time to do anything now so maybe not tonight, but if he's there tomorrow and starts arsing around again, I'll definitely do something. As I get up and take hold of the pole by the stairs, I decide to give him a stare. Shall I smile or look annoyed? Which is likely to put him off more? I haven't decided by the time I've turned to face him. The whole of the rear seat is now so dark that at first I don't see him and then, as the bus pulls up at my stop – the lamp-post at the end of my road – the upper deck is once more bathed in orange light. And I realise why I couldn't see him: he isn't there.

I stand for a moment or two before I begin to descend. As my face comes level with the floor, I scour the back of the bus. There is no-one hiding behind any seat.

Out in the clear, cool air, I watch the bus pull away, the rear windows of the upper deck in darkness. Can I see anyone sitting there? I'm really not sure any more.

3

The third night, alone at the stop in the City and here's the 109. As it approaches, there is but one thing on my mind: have they fixed those lights on the upper deck? It pulls up and instead of jumping on, I take a couple of steps back and crane my neck to look at the windows of the top deck.

When I do get on, I don't say good morning to the driver, but wave my card over the scanner. The woman in the headscarf looks up and her eyes follow me as I walk by. The LD is in full flow and for a brief moment I think I'll sit with it, but there are no seats and besides, going around in my head is something that's been with me the entire day. It's from Marcus Aurelius:

...by choosing that which is within your power, you will not be enslaved to the circumstances that surround you...

I choose and mount the stairs. The young couple has moved, no doubt to place itself in the light. It's now sitting one seat closer to my usual seat just ahead of the stairwell. Tonight, I decide to sit bang opposite the stair and thus the couple is now a matter of only two seats behind me. Perhaps that's why the smell of stale smoke appears to have increased.

I listen to hear if they are going to comment on our new seating arrangements, but they don't appear to notice or more likely, don't care. I wonder if I ought to, but it would mean turning round and I can't make that look casual enough, so I face front and open my paper. A story about graduate unemployment holds my attention until we stop. I hear the noise downstairs subside and the noise outside increase a little and looking down, I see the LD scurry off to the warrens of London Bridge Station and we pull away once more.

Behind me, the low murmur of conversation between the young couple continues, but, in spite of their proximity, I can distinguish no words. I try to read once more, but realise I've read the same passage several times before we reach the headscarf woman's stop. Will she never learn? As the bus moves off, I crane my neck to see, below and behind, that the trolley handle appears to be as stubborn as ever.

For the next few minutes, I watch my watery reflection jog up and down with me, as the bus rattles along; faster now the city's dropping behind and it's no surprise when the bus gives a particularly vicious lurch – the potholes aren't often dealt with this far out – and I'm catapulted almost out of my seat.

tinkle

I turn and the young couple notices me.

"Another one!" he says.

With something like relief, I reply,

"You'd think they'd fix them, wouldn't you? One the night before last; another last night and now this one. We'll be in total blackout soon!" The young woman looks anxious.

"D'you think so?" she asks. Fortunately, before I'm able to answer, he pipes up,

"No, mate; they fix 'em every night. When we get on, they're all working an' then one goes out. A bit later another and now this one."

This, I have not expected. I've assumed that no-one is repairing the lights, but according to this bloke, the 109 has a full complement of lights each night it sets off. The first night it lost one; the next it lost two and now it's lost three. Genuinely baffled, I say,

"But surely when it arrives at the depot with lights missing and more each night, they must realise it's more than just blown bulbs?"

"I reckon the whole wiring loom's fucked," he says.

"Well, why don't they fix it, then?" she asks and the vehemence of his reply takes me aback.

"This bus has to be twenty years old at least, you stupid cow! Not worth it, is it? Not for a few late-night losers." A pained expression flits across her face. She offers me an apologetic half-smile and snuggles up to him.

In spite of the barrenness of our exchange, I already anticipate their departure with unease. So far, the shadowy figure I thought I'd seen the last couple of nights has not put in an appearance and I find myself trying to recall at which point I become aware of his presence. Is it before the couple leaves or after? And then a thought: maybe the figure is not on the bus at all, but is in fact a collection of shadows, both inside the bus and outside it, that align in a particular way, at a particular point and in a particular light. I recall an advert on TV where the shadows thrown by a pile of junk coalesce into the shape of a car or a sofa. Or something. But that's probably CGI, isn't it?

I'm sure I've seen stuff on the internet, though: illusions, that sort of thing. People don't just appear and disappear. But then what about my paper? It didn't just spontaneously combust.

The young couple stands. Without a word, as though we had not spoken, the two of them come by me and clomp and chitter down the stairs. A split second before her eyes disappear below the guard-panel, they glance at me and their edges wrinkle, almost imperceptibly. Has she just smiled at me? Looking down, I see them emerge; he zips his jacket and, for good measure, puts his collar up and she, a second or two behind, wobbles on her heels and trots off after him. I wish; but she doesn't look up at me.

Alone.

I want to turn around, but I don't want to turn around. I'm fairly convinced by my shadow theory… fairly… but loath to test it.

"Don't be a twat," I say aloud and turn.

The street-lamps are again making the top deck glow and dim by turns. At first glance, I see there's no-one behind me and several times I allow the orange wash to bathe the rear of the bus before I am fully satisfied that I am alone. No mugger; no drunken oaf; no phantom.

I am looking towards the rear of the bus, but behind my head – that is, at the front – I almost sense it before I see it. Or hear it.

tinkle

The wiring loom's fucked

I feel the blood beat against my temple as I turn around. In the darkness that has flicked on mere feet ahead of where I sit, and framed against the front window, there is a shadow; an outline; a figure. This time, the street-lamps show me the shape of his skull. Back-lit, his long hair hangs in thin, greasy strands through which his ears may be clearly distinguished. This is no shadow.

I don't recall even *thinking* about saying it but,

"What the fuck are you playing at?" echoes around the empty deck. "Come on! What is it you want!?"

No reply. My next move ought naturally to be to stand, march forward, look him squarely in the eye and demand that he tells me what I want to know.

I remain seated. Adrenaline, produced by anger and not fear, I decide, is causing me to tremble; causing my breath to come short and rasping. Gripping the back of

the seat in front of me, I stand on shaking legs, vaguely
aware that my newspaper has fallen to the floor. I shan't
be picking it up. I want to run, but I know I can't; I want
to fling myself down the stairwell, but I know I mustn't.
Instead and slowly, keeping my eyes on the figure in the
darkness of the front seat, I descend step by step. As I set
foot on the lower deck, I am aware that the bus is
decelerating, but, peering through the windscreen, I
realise that we are still a mile or more from my stop. The
vehicle squeaks to a halt and the doors open.

"No!" I cry out to the unseen driver. "No, it's all
right. I'm not getting off; I'm just coming downstairs.
Please; there's some way to go yet." For long seconds,
all I can hear is the clatter of the diesel engine and the
rushing sound in my own ears. Then hiss, rattle, clunk
and slowly, we pull away.

4

"You've been watching that clock all night."

It's true, but not for the reason my colleague thinks. I
spent the early part of my shift wondering how I'm to
get home. During "lunch" break I sought an alternative
to the 109, but short of a cab (which I can't afford) and a
train from London Bridge, (which I can't afford) and a
taxi home at the other end (which I can't afford) there's
no way. So, for much of the second part of my shift, I'm
on auto-pilot with the callers, turning the bulk of my
thoughts to some of the calming exercises I'd discovered
doing my course.

And right now I feel fairly stoical. What's to fear? A
nutter playing tricks? Or even now, my own eyes and
tired brain doing the same. And a couple of hours back,
I even began to wonder – you know: odd visions,
hallucinations, strange smells and what have you – if I

might be developing a brain tumour. But after the exercises, even this doesn't concern me over much.

"...sick and yet happy, in peril and yet happy, dying and yet happy..." Epicetus

By the time I spot the 109 turning the corner, lightening the dark street, I'm feeling equable. It's been too long since I exercised my skills and I pride myself that in spite of this, I've not done too badly tonight.

I even greet the driver, smile at the headscarf-woman and then pull up sharp as I practically bowl into, coming down the stairs, the female constituent of the young couple. Intent on keeping herself upright on her gigantic shoes, it's not until she lands at the bottom that she looks up and notices me. She says nothing, but scuttles past, looking for a seat. She's lucky. Her position and steady gaze cause the headscarf-woman reluctantly to shuffle along and the young woman squeezes in next to the tartan trolley. Both she and I realise I'm staring. I'm wondering how to frame the question, but I don't need to.

"You can't see nothing up there," she says. "It's pitch black!"

I want to show her that she's being foolish; that I'm not afraid. But nor is he, obviously, for she's come down alone, evidently unimpressed by his lack of concern and no doubt against his wishes. If I go up, she might think I'm siding with him and I toy with the idea of trying to reassure her, but now he is standing behind me on his last, my first, step. He barges past.

"What's wrong with you, you stupid cow?" Must be a pet name. "I fuckin' warned you not to come down here. I told you, didn't I? The wiring loom's fucked! You're havin' a fuckin' laugh, leavin' me up there. What's the matter with you?" He's right in her face now.

"I'm frightened."

"What of, you soft slag?" He's yelling, but no-one's

looking except me. Her eyes flick momentarily towards mine. Is that merely accidental or is it something more? A plea? Instantly, his head jerks around. "And what the fuck are you looking at, you queer!? Jog on up them fucking stairs!"

Why doesn't someone do something? The LD is paying no attention, the driver is probably unaware and the headscarf-woman stares straight ahead of her.

I have no idea what my face tells the young woman as I go upstairs; I don't want to think about it.

But there's something wrong. As I emerge from the stairwell and look about, fully expecting several lamps to have succumbed, I'm surprised to find the entire top deck bathed in light; clear, bright light. I pause, wondering if I ought to go down and tell them, but... best not.

The wiring loom's fucked.

I take my usual seat, close to the stairwell.

I don't know how long I've been... "detained" downstairs, but it seems only minutes before the LD departs and, with a kind of normality descending, I decide to read my paper. A page or two in, I check that the headscarf-woman has managed to get away and I smile bleakly as I witness her nightly battle play out a few feet below me. The bus pulls away and I see the woman suddenly cease her struggle with the trolley and a few moments later, I sink back in my seat, the blood draining from my face.

She looked up.

She looked up at me; directly at me, like she knew exactly where I was sitting and that I'd be watching her. Never before has she looked at me – looked at *anything* save her trolley. Why did she do it and was I merely imagining the accusation in her gaze? Did she think I ought to have intervened against that loud-mouthed thug? His girlfriend must be used to it by now. If it bothered her that much, she'd have left him, wouldn't she?

Irrationally, I whisper to myself that the old bat ought to mind her own business and if she cared that much, she could have said something herself instead of just looking into the middle distance. I'm now really quite angry with her. So much for my exercises and meditations.

When the young couple gets off this time, she is in front of him. He pushes her in the back and she staggers forward. He zips his jacket and looks up at me, one finger extended. I close my eyes and breathe.

In, two, three, four, five and out, two, three, four, five and in, two, three, four, five and out, two, three, four, five and...

tinkle

My eyes spring open. To my right, a warm glow spills over the guardrail of the stairwell. Apart from this, the top deck is in darkness. I can't stay up here. It isn't just the darkness now: the air smells so strongly of diesel, of stale smoke and it tastes... old; mildewed.

Even as I set foot on the first step, the light below dims and then with each subsequent step, another lamp goes out until, as I emerge from the stairwell, the entire lower deck is dark.

My eye is caught by a vivid flash, bright, electrical, but when I look towards the source, I see nothing until another strikes through the gloom. It's coming through the small gap at the edge of the panel in the rear bulkhead, framing it in the darkness. I take a few steps towards it.

"*The wiring loom's fucked.*"

"What?!" I cry, turning.

"I said, 'the wiring loom's fucked'."

He's never said so much as a good morning to me and now he's offering this. I take a tentative step towards the cab.

"Is… is that's what's wrong with the lights?" I ask. *Another step…*

"Always is. Fucked. It's what causes them to pack up. It's what causes the fire." *And another…*

"But… but why doesn't someone fix it?" *One more…*

"Not worth it, is it? For a few late-night losers." I stop moving and for the first time hear, above me on the upper deck, the sound of footsteps. Slow, unsteady thumps and thuds, mingled with soft, dragging sounds. There was no-one up there; I know there was no-one up there. But I hear them… all of them.

They are making for the stairs, bringing the stench with them: diesel; smoke;

Fire.

And then the first hand appears inches from my face: nails melted, charred flesh black against the cold, glistening chrome of the stair rail. As it slides along, it leaves a greasy smear of brown muck.

"What's happening?" I cry. "What's happening? Stop and let me off. Now!"

"Bit difficult here, sir: nasty curve coming up. Besides, we'll be at the depot soon."

"What? It can't be. Did I miss my stop?"

"Oh no sir," he says, "Not tonight."

Flight

Charlotte Stirling

How did I find myself here? On this train with my baby daughter asleep beside me. Fleeing in a stark, dark night from my husband and brother who would take her from me.

It could happen to anyone. A wrong act here, an odd deed there. A slice of paranoia, the mention of poor mental health and you could be here too.

The sun is setting on Scotland as my train follows the coastal route towards Kings Cross and London. For once, the proud Northern Sea is brilliant cobalt, the algae collecting towards the surface sun - shimmer on a promise from Neptune. The sky looks hopeful and every mile I put between my pursuers and myself is for the better. If they catch me – all will be lost.

I gave birth to my baby only days ago. We are both newborn. Her with life and me with betrayal. It seems a lifetime has cantered between now and then. The birth of my daughter and the death of my marriage.

All the vaudevillian's are in place. The evil brother, the malicious sister-in-law, the panicked husband. The mad, bad wife.

Everybody is angry with me. I have lain in my hospital bed, the stitches pinching and bucking at every movement and nobody contacted me for days. I felt safe for a while until they spoke of taking my Rosebud to Canada to live with my brother and his hard, bitch wife. Xervantaz would like her very much. There is nothing more he enjoys than feeding of the extremes of human nature. Whether it is innocence or vitriol, he delights in the polar aspects of our extraordinary condition. He covets it, desires it and it is a demon's one source of weakness. Unlike our souls that are two a penny – it is our empathy the demonic circus really aches for.

Leaning back against the couchette, the palm of my hand laid gently on my daughter's stomach, I am reminded of better days, of cowslips, fresh lemonade and lavender days; the hum of bees succumbing to nectar and the memory of honeyed white wine. When the panicked husband cherished the mad, bad wife and I was everything to him. But how things change in the blink of a jaundiced eye.

You see, I lost the money. A lot of money. Hundreds of thousands of pounds spent on shoes, holidays, friends in need and other things over five, turbulent and sucked dry years. And we are utterly broke now. Stripped down to the very reeds. No more holidays and shoes and helping friends. No more stays in luxury hotels. No more looks of pride from my husband as I choose a delicious burgundy from a sumptuous wine list or the chateau briând just because I could. No more name dropping or boastful conversations for my husband. Just the legacy of a wasteful, mad, bad wife who lost control and used spending as a comfort.

The sun is dropping fast now in the sky and I take an exceptional solace in the shadows that ink themselves onto shore and sea. The next twelve hours are crucial.

We have to disappear from the real world and hide in the twilight for safety.

Our carriage is of the old-fashioned type with tatty doors that slide open onto the corridor and carpets of muddy green. Grey blinds are pulled all the way down the windows to protect our privacy.

I think I feel a tiny movement from the baby so I lay her down beside me and give her some room to kick and gurgle. My little rosebud. So tiny and so beautiful. The light in our carriage begins to flicker as we approach the Braid Tunnel. I rummage in my bag for something to eat because breast-feeding makes me ravenous but there isn't much. Just a quarter packet of plain biscuits, some cheddar, half a baguette and two apples. I have no money to buy anything else so this will have to do until we reach a place of greater safety.

As I take the first bite of the red apple, its sweet juices souring my mouth with hope, the carriage plunges into darkness and the stink of sulphur fills our tiny space. I reach for the baby and hold her close – not a murmur from her; she is such a good girl.

I know what to expect because this has happened before. The darkness, the stench of an unlit match, the leathery sound of old wings flapping and finally that voice made up of feces and dust, ancient and terrible suggesting depravity and painful deaths to me.

I raise my eyes and like old, clotting blood, the demon sits smugly, wings spread wide, pooling its evil before me. It's forked tongue of copper flicks and lashes towards my face and takes time with the tasting. Xervantaz has always loved my taste. He says I am like honey ice cream with a center of decay and cunts.

There's no point closing my eyes to wish him away because he will go when he's ready. These are just primary volleys until he gets into his stride. My daughter stirs and I will her to keep still. Her baby blanket is the colour of lavender and her innocence will smell too delicious to hide her for long.

Xervantaz has always loved babies.

'Lily, Lily', he whispers. 'Liver, Lilo, Lovage, Lily, Lambkin, Lingus'. I shake my head as images swarm, unwanted, into my consciousness. Terrible pictures of my Rosebud and what I might do to her in the future. Of what *he* might do.

And then, like quicksilver disappearing into the veins of a sallow-skinned addict, the train emerges from the tunnel and all that is left of my calling demon is a mound of maggots and mulch; earthy with mid-notes of death.

I let out a breath that is long and labored without the sweetness of relief. A jagged breath that constricts my lungs with tar and feathers. The mad, bad wife and her Rosebud.

Absinthe green flashes puncture the sky outside – this is Xervantaz and his curiously tender farewells.
The train begins to slow as we approach Newcastle and this makes my heart flutter like a tricolor flag at the site of Madame Guillotine. Rosebud and I are not nearly far enough away yet for my mind to cease scampering in panic.
My baby feels cold so I push her gently down my opened blouse to keep her warm. I think I hear a gurgle of contentment but the Tannoy is blaring out details of the stops and stations between here and London. I see no

sign of the demon that suggests he has others to torment and slowly strangle with fear.

Then a blue light flashes in my peripheral vision and I lean over as much as I dare to see what's happening. Policemen are marching hard towards the train. I rub my forehead, jittery and unsure of what to do next. And then I see them; the evil brother and the panicked husband striding purposefully towards me and I know it's over. For me and for my Rosebud.

My husband catches sight of me before I have time to duck back behind the window. I hear him shout, 'There!' and the footsteps get louder and harder as they pound the platform. I pull the baby towards me and breathe in as much as I can of her. These last moments will mean everything in the days to come when I am committed or worse. Held against my will in the evil brother's attic or in the cellar of the panicked husband's house.

I kiss my daughter tenderly and wait for chaos to descend. And when it does and she is wrenched from me, an oddly formed calm descends. Even the impact of my husband's palm smacking off my cheek hardly warrants a twitch. I am pulled roughly to my feet, hands twisted behind my back and manacled quickly. '*What have you done? What have you done*?' I hear my husband roar and his battle cry of grief screams its way through the ether towards me.

My Rosebud is safe from them forever. Still and pale as alabaster, her tiny blue lips, perfect for all time.

And I smile with this knowledge tucked deep in my heart.

And my demon Xervantaz smiles back from whatever Hell he resides in and the balance is restored between our worlds.

Walking Through Darkness
T.M. Hogan

CHAPTER 1

"Stop squirming!" my husband, Ben, lashes out at me. "You're making me nervous."

After a few moments of trying to keep still in front of the doctor's empty desk, I shift my weight in my seat again. I see Ben glaring at me in the corner of my eye.

"I can't help it if your unborn son won't get his foot out of my lungs," I say quietly.

Thankfully, Dr. Philip comes through the door and shuts it behind him.

"Sorry to have kept you waiting so long." He sits in his chair behind his desk, taking his time getting comfortable and sorting out the paperwork. I shake my leg and pick at my nails.

"So, Doctor." I sit on the edge of my seat, but regret it when a sharp pain shoots through my ribs and makes me lean back again. "What did the scans show?"

He opens Ben's folder and looks over his half moon glasses at my husband. "I'm sorry to tell you this, Mr. Davies, but it's not looking good."

I look at Ben and see the muscles in his face move and bulge as he clenches his jaw. I place my hand is his, "Ben, whatever it is-" He explodes, ripping his arm away from my grasp.

"For God's sake, Rebecca, can't you shut up for five minutes?! I'm trying to find out if I'm fucking dying here and all you can do is yabber on!"

I choke as I begin to cry, sniffing back the tears that always seem to be there waiting behind my eyes lately.

"Mr. Davies, please calm down. You will need the support of your wife and loved ones in the coming months," Dr. Philip says in a calming voice. "Mrs. Davies, my only comfort is that these recent violent and uncharacteristic outbursts your husband has been having are symptoms of the illness." He lets out a loud breath before turning back to Ben. "I'm sorry to tell you this... you have stage four cancer. A tumour the size of a golf ball is growing inside the left hemisphere of your brain."

Both Ben and I are stunned silent. I want to ask questions, but fear the repercussion of my husband.

"How long do I have left?" Ben's voice quavers.

"Untreated, you are looking at three months, maybe six, maybe more. There's really no saying in these sorts of things. Tumours often act completely independent to medical guidelines, but my best judgement isn't very long."

"And if treated?" I ask.

"There are a range of paths we can take. I wouldn't bother with any long term treatments. My professional opinion is that you take the most aggressive option of treatment as soon as possible. That will include radiotherapy and chemotherapy along with a cocktail of drugs tailored to your specific needs."

Ben goes silent and stares off at nothing again. I sit back and rest my hands on my swollen belly. What am I going to do? Fight this, of course. With what money? Ben and I will find a way. Oh, just when everything was going so well...

"Mrs. Davies, how long until you're due?"

"Oh, I'm thirty-two weeks pregnant." I give him a small smile. "It's our first. We've lost two before to miscarriages."

"I'm sorry to hear that." His eyes are full of compassion and understanding.

I wish I could break down and cry, I wish I could get a hug from him. Ben's illness has come as a rude shock, an unpleasant surprise, and during what is meant to be the most blessed time of our lives together.

"We will do our best to beat this disease," Dr Phillip says with a smile.

CHAPTER 2

The red ball of energy blasts towards me, the centre so hot and fierce it glows white. I block it with my hand, sending sparks everywhere hurling the ball in the opposite direction. It lands somewhere among the shrubbery and instantly sets the bush on fire.

"Good work, Suriel," Elemiah says, clapping her hands as she approaches me. "I think it's safe to say, after a decade of working with me, you are finally ready to set off on your own."

A swirl of excitement bubbles in my belly.

"What do you think? Are you ready to set off into the Netherworld on your own?"

I look down at the Death Witch. She is smaller than me and thousands of years older. Her appearance is misleading. In the human world she wears the cloak of a handsome tall woman. In reality she can snuff out one's life with a whisper, not to mention her true form is the thing of nightmares.

"Yes, I believe I'm ready to travel the Nether."

"Good." She walks away from me. "I'm off to a feast." She disappears in a whirlwind of magic, her laugh still rings through the air.

"Ugly old hag."

Being on my own again after ten years of forced

companionship, I feel like a child free to roam the streets without the watchful eye of her parents. I begin walking with no real purpose through the ever dark Netherworld. There is no sun here, no moon or stars to see by. An endless darkness fills this realm and I must rely on my keen senses to guide me safely over rocks and plants. Seconds pass into minutes, minutes into hours. I come upon no greater life forms in my travels. A few insects here and there, some spirits that reside in the ethereal energies of the universe.

Out of nowhere, a pain rips through my flesh and I fall to my knees. I look down and see a spear embedded in my calf just above the ankle. The rope attached to the end of the spear is pulled taut as I am dragged along the barren rocky ground. I swallow the screams before they escape my mouth and see a demon looming before me.

"Ah, I have struck fresh meat," a low guttural voice booms from his body. He is tall, over six feet, a body of hot black brimstone. His eyes and mouth glow with a fiery orange whenever he opens them. I slide beneath him as he leans over me. "Lovely, succulent flesh." I squirm with agony as he pulls at the rope. "Tonight I will be satisfying more than one of my carnal pleasures."

Wrapping his enormous hand around my throat, he pulls me up to eye level and inhales my scent.

"Mmm, you smell human."

"Spare me." I choke out. What passes as a face moves. "Spare me. I'll strike a bargain with you."

"What could you possibly offer me that I can't get myself?"

I fight to speak, but can barely breathe in enough air to fill my lungs. He drops me to the ground and I scream as I land on my harpooned calf.

"It's difficult for you to find fresh meat here. What living creatures roam these lands? When was the last time you had flesh like mine to devour?"

This stops the demon and he quietens in thought.

"What is your name, human?"

"My name is Suriel, and I do not know what makes you think I am human, for I am a Demon Witch."

He leans down so his head is above mine and takes a deep breath through his nose. "Well, you smell human, if only a bit." I stare at him, confused.

"So, what say you, demon. I bring you another fresh morsel for you to devour and you let me on my way?"

"NO!" His voice slams against my chest and rattles my ears. He takes a moment before speaking. "I require three sacrifices, young virile humans, men and women in their primes."

"I can bring them to you."

"That is not all. You may leave here after you bring them to me, but you are not free forever. You are to finish repaying your debt to me in the future."

"Who are you to demand so much? You are a pig! Instead of one scrawny Witch you will be getting three humans in their prime, and you dare to demand more!"

"SILENCE! I am the demi-god Harahel! You will do as I say, or I will eat you where you stand."

A shudder runs through me, but I stand my ground.

"Bring me three humans in their prime; then, when the time is right, I will be coming for you."

"And what exactly do you plan to do with me and when?"

"Fifty years – you will pay me with your body and soul."

I fold my arms and tap my foot. "Fine, where will I bring the meat?"

"Come back to the Netherworld with them, and I will find you," before I can react, he slams his palm into my forehead, "with this." I stagger backward rubbing my head. "You are now bound to me by contract. Nothing can break it but the King of Hell."

CHAPTER 3

I hold the straw to Ben's lips. "Drink, you need to keep your fluids up."

He hits my arm back, making the water splash onto his lap. "Now look what you have done!" he yells.

I cringe back into my seat as everyone in the room turns to stare at us, clutching the cup to my chest as my abdomen tightens all over.

"I'm sorry," I say to him quietly, "I didn't mean to upset you."

We're in the hospital today, for one of Ben's many chemo treatments. So far the meds seem to be helping to shrink the tumour. We're hoping to get it small enough to operate, but it hasn't been helping his temperament. The Ben that sits half dead beside me is nothing like the man I married and fell in love with. I move the pillow behind me into a better position as another Braxton-Hicks, practice contractions before labour, tightens my belly.

"God, please don't let this baby come now."

"What's wrong?" Ben snaps.

"These contractions are becoming really annoying, and frequent. I just hope it's not a sign of the baby coming. We're not ready."

"You'd better hope it doesn't come now, because I won't stay in the house and listen to the meat bag crying all damn day and night."

I turn away from him as tears run down my face.

CHAPTER 4

The Fire Elemental places its hand on my chest and

begins chanting. Instant pain bursts through me and I scream. Searing heat burns through my lungs and my bones feel like iron plunged into the fires of hell. My screaming is snuffed and my throat is seared by flames. I am trapped in the most painful experience of my life and I begin to contemplate death; but it is not an option, I must endure this. All I can hear is the Elemental's ethereal voice over the searing crackle of heat, and feel the fire spreading through every vein in my body.

Finally, I am released from its enchantment and collapse to the ground. As I rest with my head between my knees, I see the flicker of its flame disappear from the molten floor. Slowly, I push myself up and sit on my feet, examining the changes. First, I notice the hair hanging over my face has turned from light brown to pitch black, and then I see a new addition to my arms. The veins have been burnt black, making a striking contrast against my porcelain skin. My nails have thickened almost claw-like, a faded black. Now that the pain has gone, I feel the new power I have acquired for the price of my soul.

"I see what you are doing, Suriel." Elemiah's voice comes unexpectedly from behind me. I get to my feet and turn to her. "You've been making a lot of contracts with your soul as the price. What, you didn't think I'd find out?"

I keep silent and turn as she slowly circles me. She mocks me and her eyes shine deadly. "You think that it'll end in a blood bath, all your buyers fighting to the death for your little soul!" She barks out a laugh. "Oohh, how wrong you are. It'll merely be shredded into equal parts, and you will suffer so much more than you would have under my complete control. Stupid girl."

My heart pumps frantically in my chest, but I keep my face blank. I'm not letting that hag get the best of me.

"Let me give you a little tip, for old time's sake." Elemiah walks up to me casually and I take a step back. She picks up a lock of my hair and rubs it between her thumb and forefinger. "The only one that can break all your contracts is Ragul, The King of Hell!" Her eyes light up and she bursts out, laughing. "Good luck getting an audience with him, dear."

CHAPTER 5

The midwife grasps my arms firmly, lightly pulling me from Ben's bed.

"Rebecca, you need to get to the birthing suite now. We need to check on the baby."

"Nooo," I moan in protest, "I can't, not yet, he isn't ready yet."

"It's okay, sweetie, the baby is developed enough to come out safely." I'm not sure if I meant my baby or my husband. "Come now, we'll take perfect care of you and the baby." Another contraction makes me bend over in pain.

15, 16, 17....

they're getting longer and closer together.

"I know, but Ben needs me."

"Mrs. Davies, Ben is in the best of hands." Dr. Philip kneels before me so we're at eye level. "My team of highly-trained medical staff and I will be with him the entire time. We're going to take him into theatre shortly to operate on the tumour. I hope for Ben to greet his newborn son when he awakes." Dr. Philip's smile beams through the strains of hair hanging over my eyes.

I breathe heavily through another contraction. "Okay, I'll go," I say, defeated. I lean over Ben and kiss him softly on his freshly shaved head. The chemo has made the tumour small enough to operate on and he's already been put to sleep with drugs. "Good luck, my love, see you on the other side." Be it in life or death.

Once I'm sitting in the wheelchair, I'm pushed to the maternity ward and into the birthing suite. I never imagined I would be giving birth like this – alone, stressed, with an abusive and insane husband about to go into life-threatening surgery. I don't know if I can handle this.

"You're six centimetres," the midwife says as she takes her hand out of me.

The pain is excruciating. How long will it be before I need to push?

Minutes turn into hours. Hours pass into the next day.

"You're six, maybe seven, centimetres."

"What?" I scream. "I've been going at this for hours. Only one centimetre?"

"I'm sorry, I'll speak with the doctors." The midwife turns to leave.

"Wait! How is my husband doing? Is he out of surgery yet?" She turns to face me.

"I will check for you."

I rest my head on my arms as another contraction brings me to my knees.

Sitting in the wheelchair again I'm placed beside Ben. He got out of surgery a couple of hours before me. My natural birth had turned into an emergency caesarean. I am now freshly showered and holding our baby son, Matthew.

"Hey, Becky," Ben's old, sweet voice greets me. I smile up to his still sleepy face, tears of happiness reflected in his eyes.

"Hi." I choke on my words. "Matthew, say hello to daddy." I try to raise my arms to show Ben, but pain radiates through my abdomen.

"Here, let me help you with that," a nurse says as she

comes over and helps bring Matthew into Ben's arms.

"Hey, little man, it's great to finally meet ya." Ben's eyes shine with love and happiness and I know the surgery was a success. I have my husband back.

CHAPTER 6

The gates of Hell loom before me, standing as giant black sentinels. They need no guards. The real danger lies within. It has taken many years to get here, making deals and contracts leaving me deep in pools of blood. The carnage I have wrought in my endeavours has made my name known far and wide in the Netherworld.

I am emotionally exhausted; the strain of completing the contracts has drained my energy to the breaking point. I only hope I can persuade the King to want my soul badly enough to buy it and break all existing contracts. With many of my contracts coming to an end in five years, it's the last chance I have.

"I've been waiting for you, Suriel," a masculine voice fills the cavern with a rumble. The room was hollowed out over millennia by magma that still flows behind the throne. I walk slowly, feigning confidence as I make my way across the ledge in the wall.

"I am honoured that you would have me in your presence, oh King of Hell."

"Whispering of your journey through the Netherworld reached my ears many years ago. It has been interesting to say the least, watching your growth."

That was unexpected. "You flatter me, Ragul... may I call you that?" Coming down to the main floor, I make my way towards the dais that holds the throne. Ragul, the King of Hell, is monstrously large. Standing up, I imagine, he'd be the height of a four-story building.

"You may." His deep, rich voice rumbles through the

cavern again. "Tell me, what is it you want from me, Suriel? Trying to make another sale?"

"As a matter of fact, yes. I want you to break all my existing contracts, all thirteen of them. I want you to be the one and only owner of my soul."

"Give me one reason why I shouldn't kill you where you stand?" There's no way to read any emotion on his metallic face. Who knows what he truly looks like beneath all that metal?

"Because, I offer you more than just my soul. I will give you my body and mind to do with as you wish." I drop to one knee before him and bow. "I am your servant. You have complete control over me. Ask me anything and it shall be done, for all eternity." My head feels light and heavy all at once as my heart pumps frantically in my chest.

"And one thousand innocent souls."

I look up at him. "What?"

"I'll take your servitude, in addition to one thousand innocent souls."

My eyes dart left and right, then stop at his feet. "When do you want them by?"

"There is no time limit. Harvest those souls for me, and when you are done, I will decide then if I choose to follow through with the deal. If you do not wish to go through with the deal, then may we never cross paths again."

"Yes, my King," I bow low once more, "I will harvest those souls for you."

CHAPTER 7

The baby is crying again. Long cries turn into high-pitched screams. I cram my hands over my ears as Matthew wails. Tears stream down my face. The thought of smothering the baby with a pillow flashes through my mind and I am horrified I could think such a thing, which only brings on a fresh wave of tears.

"Rebecca! Shut that fucking baby up," Ben's voice rumbles through the house.

I hiccup and drag myself over to Matthew's crib, lifting him out and holding him to my chest like a lifeline.

"You useless whore! You wanted a baby so badly and you're too lazy to look after it. You piece of shit thinking you could be a mother. You're the worst mother I've ever met!"

I shut my eyes as if that will shut out his cruel words. He's right. I know he's right. I'm a horrible mother. It'd be better for all of us if I just killed myself or left. Then he'd have a better woman raise my child. I'm just damaging him. The tiny tumours that have bloomed all through Ben's brain will kill him in a few short weeks. Maybe I should try to cope until he's gone, maybe I'll get better, or maybe I'll just get worse...

CHAPTER 8

The portal between here and the human world closes behind me. The dim light from the apartment's TV pops out of existence and the street sounds cease to exist. I stumble through the forest of the Netherlands in an area I've claimed as my own. The images playing through my mind don't help me navigate the thick fog and maze of hidden tangled roots.

I passed through the portal feeling optimistic; this was to be my five hundredth kill, my half way mark of reaping the innocent souls for Ragul. I'd had my eye on this cosy family for a week, sussing them out. It never takes me long to decide on which infants are right for the picking and which I should detour. I am drawn to them without any effort on my part.

I bend over the crib and lift the creature up into my arms, pressing it to my chest like a loving mother. The red ethereal light coming from the portal behind me cloaks its face in fiery hues.

"Get away from my baby!" a hysterical female voice screams.

I look up and see the mother standing outside the baby's room in the hallway. She makes her way towards me, dressed only in a flimsy robe. Her breast pops out in her haste.

"Stop." I give a single command and she stops in her tracks. All fight drains from her body, but the fear and pain never leave her watery eyes. I look down and make coddling noises to the babe.

"What are you going to do to my baby?" the mother asks in a strangled whisper.

My burning eyes look up to her. "I'm going to kill it." I pull out my long, curved dagger and place it under the baby's chin. Not once has it roused from its peaceful slumber, nor shall it ever. I only have to press ever so gently for the deadly sharp metal to break the supple flesh and drag the blade across its throat, severing the vocal chords and opening the arteries. The fresh crimson blood pools in my arm before draining to the floor.

Slowly, the ringing in my ears ebbs away and I'm left to contend with the mother's wailing screams of anguish. I walk to her and gently lay her limp child's body in her arms, as if I still have to worry about rousing the sleeping child. Her arms tremble as her body shudders from the heart wrenching pain I've subjected her to.

"Come, sit down." I lead the mother with her only child to the rocking chair in the corner of the room. She sits down and rocks out of habit. The baby, with the bloody smile under her chin, rests her head against her mother's bosom. "Here," I hand her my dagger. "Cut deep, down like this." I lightly run my nail down the inside of her forearm. She looks at me in confusion, hiccupping as she tries to understand what I am implying. "You will never recover from this. You will never bring another child into this world. You will only make others suffer if you continue on." I wrap my hands around her hand grasping the handle of my dagger. "End your life so you may join your child in the afterlife."

Her tears have stopped. The well is dry. Her eyes resolute as they turn from mine and look at her exposed wrist. Pressing the tip into her wrist, she drags it down, opening a twenty centimetre gash that quickly pours out blood.

"And the other."

She switches hands and presses the blade into her wrist, opening an identical wound on her right arm.

"That's it," I pull the dagger from her hand and put it back in its sheath behind my back whilst stroking the hair out of her eyes. She leans back and rests her head on the pillow, rocking her baby as her life force drains away.

Leaving the empty shells behind me, I pass through the portal into the Netherworld.

Lost in memory I trip again and catch myself on one of the tree beside me. I hear heavy breathing behind me and turn to see fire and stone bounding towards me.

"I've come to collect your debt."

"You're three years premature, Harahel."

"I come when I want," he says as he stands before me.

"Yes, that's what they all say."

He looks at me confused.

I roll my eyes, turn, and walk away. "Fuck off."

I hear the twigs and dry leaves crunching behind me.

"Who do you think you are speaking to me like that? I am the demi-god Harahel. You sold me your soul and I am here to collect! No one ignores Harahel!"

Just before his arm swoops down upon me I turn around again and place my hand on the glowing ember in the centre of his chest. Heat races up my arm as I suck all the life force out of him. He's dumb-struck by the sudden power I wield as he slowly dies under my hand. My hand glows bright, illuminating his now dark face.

"You should never have underestimated me, for it has been a long time since we met, demi-god Harahel."

Once the last morsel of life-force has left his body and entered mine, he crumples to the ground in a heap of blackened stones and coal. "Hah," I laugh to myself. "And you called yourself a demi-God?" I step over his remains and continue on my way. "Weak."

CHAPTER 9

Dr. Philip squeezes my shoulder. "He's been in a coma for two weeks now. His vital signs are decreasing steadily, Mrs. Davies. I suggest you say your good byes to him now."

I hold onto Ben's hand as I stroke our son's hair. Since Ben has been in hospital I've been laying Matthew on his chest, so they can sleep together. It's the only peace we get as a family now. "So, you truly believe this is it, this is the time?"

"It's a surprise he's held on this long, but all the signs show that he has only hours to live, at the most, until morning." As Dr. Philip walks out the door, a loud beeping comes from one of the many machines keeping Ben alive.

"What's going on?" I stand and turn to the doctor as he strides back in to look at the monitor. He presses a button and the sound stops. Panic grips my heart. "Doctor?"

"I'm sorry, Rebecca." He holds my gaze and says nothing more.

I look at the monitor in disbelief. His heart rate has dropped dramatically. I take in a shaky breath as my throat tightens. "Oooh, Ben." I can't stop myself from crying. I bury my face into the nook of his arm and let the hospital robes soak up my tears. A single high note rings through the room signalling the end of Ben's life. "Nooo!!"

Matthew starts crying loudly into my ear. It fades as someone pulls him off Ben's chest. I feel hands on me, but I don't register anyone else in the room. There's only Ben. But he's gone now. I have nothing. These bodiless hands take me away from my Ben. People speak to me and I nod here and there. I sign where they tell me to. The nurse places a bottle filled with pills in my hand, her eyes are wide and her mouth is moving. I nod some more and reassure her, just so she can leave me alone. I know I'm conscious but it feels like a dream, my senses aren't registering what's happening around me. I'm locked in the darkness of my mind. I've lost the love of my life, the man of my dreams, the father of my child. I've lost everything.

"Here." Someone lifts my hand and places a paper cup into it. "Drink this with your pills. You'll feel better."

I don't know what the pills are for but I put two in my mouth and drink the cup of water as I am ordered to.

"Mrs. Davies, I think it's time you went home to get some sleep. There are no more bottles or nappies in your bag for the baby and he'd be better off in his crib anyway. You both need to rest."

"Yes." My eyes are dry, all the tears are gone. I feel parched. "I'll get going then." I turn and walk towards the elevator.

"Mrs. Davies!" I stop and turn.

"Your baby." The nurse looks concerned. "He's in the nursery."

"Oh yes, mustn't forget the baby." I turn and walk to the nursery. The nurse asks if there's anyone she can contact to pick me up but I tell her again I have no other family. I pick up Matthew and the nappy bag, and make my way to the car as the sun just begins to brighten the sky. Putting Matthew in his seat I dump the bag on the floor, slam the door shut and slump behind the steering wheel. Turning the key in the ignition, I drive off into the dawn.

The roads are quiet. It's Sunday, so none of the usual morning traffic, which is probably a really good thing because I've been changing lanes without indicating and I don't stop at any stop sign. I have no energy in me to care right now. I just want to get home and fall into bed. Hopefully, Matthew will be content with holding his own bottle. I think of his little hands struggling to hold the big bottle in place. I feel no warmth in my heart as I snigger at the image.

A car horn blares as I drive past. I am grateful for the drugs the hospital gave me. I feel nothing. Lights zip past me in a blur. The pain of Ben's death isn't there anymore. The sky is slowly getting lighter; through the window I see shades of royal blue, wisps of clouds with golden and pink hues. Red lights pass the edge of my vision. I'll miss Ben, the way he held me in his strong arms. Blinding bright headlights fill my window now. The smell of his cologne. Glass explodes into my face as something huge crashes through the windshield, breaking my body. I'm pounded back again as another brute force sends the car into a tail spin.

Darkness awaits me.

CHAPTER 10

Cars speed past, their lights filtering through the trees where I conceal myself at the edge of the woods. An overturned car braces against the trees. One headlight survived and illuminates the people coming to aid the occupants. But no aid will be needed. The driver is dead, her infant son gone too, but his soul won't be joining her in the afterlife. He gets a one way ticket to Ragul.

Branches groan as they bend, twigs crack as they snap and the clicking of joints fills the air above me. I look up and see a giant bloated spider poised above me. Her distorted human head smiles down at me, poisonous saliva gleaming on her metal teeth.

"So nice of you to join me in the human world, Elemiah." I look back down at the crash scene. An ambulance has arrived.

"I see you're still doing the handy work of others." Elemiah's warped form slowly floats down to me as she spins her thread from the branch above. "Or are you going to tell me this is what you do for fun now?" Her hideous face stops inches away from mine, staring at me with her eight beady eyes.

"What I do in my spare time is none of your concern."

"That may be." One claw gathers a lock of my hair and she breathes me in deeply. "But it's not long now." She giggles and a deep gurgle rattles in her chest. "In only a short time, I will be here again to gobble you up." Without warning she encases me in all eight of her legs and buries her face into my neck. "Oh, how I've longed to bite into your supple flesh, that innocent soul of yours that is somehow still so human." Her long rough tongue slides up my face. "Until then, my sweet." She releases me as swiftly as she pounced on me and clatters off into the night.

I finally let my body relax and a shudder runs all the way through me.

Only ten left to go, and then I will be free – well, as free as a slave to the King of Hell can be, anyway. If Elemiah weren't so strong I would have disposed of her and avoided all this mess.

CHAPTER 11

After a while of staring at the nurse taking notes on my chart, I clear my throat to speak. She jumps, startled by the sound. I watch her as if in slow motion while she composes herself to appear professional again.

"You're awake."

"I'm awake."

"How are you feeling?" I have to stop to think about that one. How do I feel? I feel nothing.

"Empty." She pats my hand, then squeezes gently.

"It's probably the drugs. You've been through a lot. You've been sedated quite a bit since the accident."

I swallow the lump in my throat. "Accident?"

A look of concern warps her features again. "I'll go get the doctor for you."

I lie back and stare at the blank TV. Slowly, I begin to register my injuries. I can only see through a small slit in my right eye, it's swollen and painful. When I open and close my mouth a wound is torn afresh. Just breathing hurts; with every rise of my chest a sharp pain shoots through my side. I guess that's what a broken rib feels like. I can't remember what happened to me, but its there, just behind the veil. I'm not ready to remember what I've done. I know it's bad. I can see the shape of one foot under the blankets, but the other side is flat. I turn my leg but the blanket doesn't shift. I shake my leg more vigorously and regret it as I bang the stump against the railings. I scream out in pain and breathe heavily; I don't want to be sedated again. Instead, I throw the blankets away and reveal my right leg, the thigh remains but what used to be my knee and below is gone.

I grip the railings tightly with both hands. My ears ring and my stump throbs. This is the price I paid... paid for... for crashing the car. Oh, God, I crashed the car. What happened to the others involved? Did I kill anyone? Am I a murderer now? Oh, what about my son, what about Matthew?

Dread floods my body and suddenly I'm filled with adrenaline, the need to fight, the need to see my son and know he's ok. I can't be left alone in this world!

A doctor walks into my room, followed by the nurse that was here before.

"Rebecca, it's good to see you awake, how are you feeling?" he says softly.

"Just tell me, please, just tell me. My son, is he alright? The crash, I remember the crash, was anyone else hurt? Please, please tell me nobody died!" My voice breaks.

"A driver died at the scene, a passenger en route to the hospital; two others are in critical condition, one has already left the hospital." He pauses and looks at me sorrowfully.

"Please, my son, tell me..." He slowly shakes his head. Before he opens his mouth I know what he is going to say. I fall back into my pillow and pull at my hair.

"I'm sorry, Rebecca. Your son died instantly. He wasn't strapped into his seat." My heart skips a beat as the scene passes through my mind, putting him into the baby seat and shutting the door, no memory of strapping him in securely.

"Naahhooo, nooo noo nooooooo." My voice comes

out croaky and strained from the lump in my throat. My chest is about to burst the guilt seizing every part of my body. No amount of physical injuries could eclipse the pain of my heart.

I wake alone at night in my hospital room. They must have sedated me again.

"You are not alone," a sweet voice comes from the corner of the room. A tall majestic figure walks out of the shadows and stands by my bed. The single light in the room is directly above them, leaving their face in shadow as light radiates around them, like an angel.

"What do you want?" My voice is flat. Empty.

The figure strokes the loose strands of hair from my face, watching as my hair slides between their fingers and onto my shoulder. The voice is odd. I can't tell if it's female or male. "Oh, there's nothing I want. I'm here for you. I'm here to take away all your pain and suffering." But as the figure fully faces me, I see it as female.

"I have lost everything. My husband, the love of my life, taken away too soon by cancer, and my son, my newborn baby, died because of my recklessness. There's nothing you can do for me."

"My child, you do not know whom you speak to. I am an Angel and I can make you reborn. This suffering will end, and you will live under my wing as a soldier of mine."

I stare at her. "But, but why me? I deserve to die. Why come to me instead of one of the innocent souls that I killed?" She looks at me sadly.

"They are already gone and have no penance. But you, my sweet, there is much work you can do for me."

"What's the price?"

"Oh, there is no price."

"There's always a catch." Feeling empty and already half way through death's door, I really don't care what the stakes are, I'll do anything to end this pain I'm in and make the score equal for the pain I've caused and the lives I've taken.

"You will help me in the afterlife for a while, and when the time is up, I will..." her voice trails off as if in thought, "cleanse your soul." Well, that doesn't sound too bad.

"Fine, it's a deal. I don't care what happens anymore." She smiles brightly at me, suddenly looking sinister. "By the way, what's your name?"

"Elemiah."

CHAPTER 12

Standing outside Hell's gates, Elemiah waits alone in all her horrific glory.

"Why are you here?" I ask her.

"To collect your soul, your time is up." She hisses back at me.

I look at my wrist pretending to check the time, though there are no clocks in the Netherworld. "Ooo, sorry Elemiah, still a few more hours until then." I walk past her and push the gate open enough for me to slide through. "Besides, I don't think Ragul would be too happy with you killing his next appointment." As the gate closes behind me I hear her final words.

"We'll see about that."

Ragul's eyes follow me as I casually make my way to the throne.

"You have collected the souls?"

I get down on both knee and bow. "I have, Your Majesty. All one thousand souls of the innocent, reaped just for you."

A loud, metallic clatter comes from his direction, screaming metal as a door swings open. I look up and see a pale masculine figure coming towards me from Ragul's giant metal body.

"Stand," he says in a deep, manly voice. "That's just an impressive piece of armour." He gestures at the giant metal body still sitting straight in the throne.

I look back down to soak up the true image of my King. His skin is pale white, almost transparent. His eyes are as black as the abyss, with a thin ring of white as an iris. Yet, his lips are the most succulent shade of red and lusciously full. He wears nothing other than a one shouldered, blood red robe.

"So, you have fulfilled your end of the bargain, it would seem. Now, do I accept?"

"I can only hope so, Your Majesty."

"What was it again that you proposed? Your soul, to break all those other contracts you had made." He looks at me deviously. "And I do so remember you offering your body to me as well."

"Whatever the King pleases, shall be his. I offer anything and everything willingly." He smirks.

"I accept."

I take the time to soak in the relief of this moment. For sixty years I ran around the Netherworld doing the bidding of others, fearing for my life, but more importantly, the final resting place of my soul. To go to Elemiah would have meant an eternity of suffering. Going with Ragul may not be any different but it doesn't seem as daunting as being left with the monster that started me on this downward spiral. The pain I felt as Rebecca would pale in comparison. I thought that was anguish, but being under Elemiah's control would mean living that pain over and over again, magnified a thousand times with no end and no escape. "Oh, thank you so much, Ragul!" I had barely finished my sentence as his hand plunges into my chest, what's left in my lungs escaping me.

Ragul holds my head attentively, then rips my heart from my chest, holding it up between us still beating, as my life slowly ebbs away. "Thank you for all you have done, Suriel. Your suffering has come to an end as I take your heart," he turns his hand, "your body," he jolts me gently, "and your soul."

I expect him to kiss me, but he stops short from pressing his lips to mine. My world begins to darken and my soul is sucked out of my body.

Wrath Of A Limbless God

William Douglas Frank

Lost in the unceasing flames,
I wait for the compassionate touch of my hangman.
Isolated beneath the radiant darkness of the morning star,
I laugh with your innocent memories as I am swallowed by the searing sands.
Fading into emptiness, a disheveled prisoner in a rusty can.
Before me are the ashes of heaven's front door...
even God is damned.
Forgotten by all who worshiped my power,
I conjure the death of a promised land...

Cake & Quill

Never Again

J. Cassidy

Jo leaned against the hallway wall, watching while her mum pinned the life-like drawing of a raven to her front door beside the picture of Isis, only half listening to her chatter. She grunted when her mum turned to stare at her, finished with her task.

"Ravens were always thought of as being creatures of darkness, bringers of death. But that couldn't be further from the truth."

"No?" Jo asked, uninterested, but she didn't want to hurt her mum's feelings.

"They come in the darkness and clean away the filth left over. Guide those on the cusp from this world to the next. It'll guide you while you go from one life to another..."

"I haven't died." She didn't mean to sound as abrupt. Her mum gave her a sad smile and cupped her cheek before stepping away to reach for her coat on the hooks she had installed before putting up the raven.

"I like that one," Jo pointed to Isis. Her mum hummed.

"Well, I thought, what's guidance without wisdom? I'll come by tomorrow with some shopping. I've left you some money so you can order in for tonight."

"You didn't need to."

"I did." Her mother paused by the front door, leaving it half-open, and stared again with watery eyes. Jo swallowed, tears forming in her own. Her mum came back in and wrapped her arms around her for several seconds before returning to the door.

"He's gone. He won't ever come back," she said. Jo wondered whose benefit that reassurance was for.

"Good night. I'll see you tomorrow."

The door closed with a thud, rattling the badly fitted light bulb out of its socket. Jo swore as the hallway was plunged into darkness, and groped along the wall, feeling ahead with her feet to avoid the glass. She wished she had taken the time to sort it before it got dark but there had been so much to do with the unpacking and then her mother had stopped by. She had been more upset than Jo, wailing and blaming herself for everything he'd done. It had taken an entire pot of tea to calm her down.

She reached the kitchen and felt around for the light switch, then blinked when yellow glare flooded the room. Her heart skipped a beat after she saw him coming up the hallway from the corner of her eye. Of course he wasn't really there. It was just memories; her mind playing tricks.

She sang to herself while she rutted around the drawers for the light bulbs, tensing as she saw the shadow sweep up behind her. She sang louder, swinging round when it reached her shoulder. Nothing there, again. The words to the song she didn't really like much came in gasps and she leaned on the bench, heart pounding. She grabbed a stool from under the table then pushed the kitchen door open, trying to get as much light as she could out into the hallway. It glinted on the sharp edges of the thin glass which would splinter in her foot all too easily if she were to step on it. She wished she'd thought of putting her shoes on but they were sitting by the front door.

It was the work of a few moments to position the stool and climb up, then grab the hanging light to steady herself while she tried to get the bulb into place. It slipped through her fingers as a banging boomed throughout the flat. She paused, the crack of the bulb when it smashed into the floor lost in the noise that she finally realised was coming from the door.

"Who's that?" she called, to receive another knock in reply. With care, she got down from the stool and stepped around the glass. The drawing of the raven watched her approach.

"It's just someone at the door. Nothing more."

Telling herself so wasn't as reassuring as singing, but she didn't want to look like some sort of lunatic to whoever was there. The picture of the raven fluttered when the knocking sounded again, the door handle vibrating in her palm with the force of it. She yanked the door open.

"What's with the...." her voice trailed off. Taking a few steps into the corridor, Jo peered around the corner to the other flats on her floor. There was no one around, the door to the stairwell firmly closed. She shivered. Someone had left the corridor window open. It was the middle of December and though there was no snow yet, it felt as if there would be soon.

"Very mature!" she called over her shoulder, going back inside. She edged round the glass, toward the front room and hit the light switch. The sweeping brush was where Mum had left it, propped against the window right next to where he was peering through.

Jo did a double take, pressing her hand over her heart. There was nothing there. There couldn't be. She was on the second floor.

"Leave me alone!" she called through the glass anyway. It was just like before, when she was only starting to realise that he was about. It had begun with him staring at her through her windows. A few days later she closed the curtains and had left them shut since. The sole reason she had chosen this flat was because she didn't want to have to go through that again.

She shivered. Sinking onto the settee, Jo wrapped her arms around herself, letting out a sob. He was there, at the other end of the long room, leaning against the wall just like the last time she had seen him.

A few moments before the last time she'd seen him.

"I didn't mean to kill you. I just wanted you to go away."

He didn't answer, didn't move at all. Jo frowned, realising that what she had been looking at was a couple of boxes with a few blankets draped over them.

"Everyone said it was self-defence!" she called, hugging herself tighter. She shuffled around on the couch as a shiver ran down her spine, and pressed her back into the cold leather. It felt marginally safer, but not safe enough. She got up and grasped the broom, holding it like a weapon, and advanced on the hallway. She left the door wide, adding to the light coming from the kitchen.

The glass was swept to the side in a single stroke. Her eyes rested on the picture of the raven, just visible in the dim light. The page fluttered in the breeze coming from under the door. It made it look as though it were flying out of the paper.

"I hear the girl who had this place before me could have used you. She did herself in only a couple of weeks ago. Police think it was a pact with some guy that lived on the ground floor. Do you do suicide cases?"

Did it do mental cases, she wondered to herself, turning away.

"Never again." The deep, croaky voice sent an electric bolt from her scalp to her toes. Her body stiffened. She closed her eyes and took a deep breath, mentally urging herself to run. If only she had a back door to escape. Reluctantly she opened her eyes, to see nothing.

"I'm hearing things now." And talking to herself, she noted as she began singing again. Strange though, that it should answer her with such clarity.

Leaving the broom propped up next to the glass she had swept into the wall, she jogged back to the front room and threw herself on the settee. Seeing the two ten pound notes her mum had left, Jo picked up the phone and dialled her local pizza place, puzzled when she realised there was no dial tone. It took a moment to remember she wasn't connected yet. She took the money and went back to the hallway, grabbing her coat as she passed it, then stopped when she saw the raven staring at her.

"Think I'll be safe out there on my own? He is gone. They're taking me seriously now. The police said I could call their Victim Support thingy. I'd need a working phone for that, though."

The gap under her door was too large, letting in the wind blowing through the open corridor windows. The light came through too, disturbed by the shadows of a pair of feet. She paused in the act of reaching for the handle and backed away.

"He's still here. He's still following me. Everywhere I went, there he was and no one ever listened. And he still won't go away and still no one is listening."

"Never again."

The raven's beak hadn't moved but the deep, cracking voice had come from the door without a doubt. She shook herself off. Whoever was on the other side had obviously spoken. Taking a deep breath, she thrust a hand into her coat pocket and wrapped her fingers around the cold metal knuckles she had taken to carrying, and jerked the door open. It banged off her hallway wall, revealing exactly nothing on the other side.

"You're too easily amused!" she called into the hallway and let the door slam shut. She slid down the wall, her eyes going to the picture of the raven.

"I thought you were supposed to be for guidance."

"Never again."

There was no more uncertainty. It was the raven who had spoken, as unmoving as it was. A violent shiver went through her.

"You're supposed to guide me 'from one life to another'. You aren't supposed to guide him back from the dead. Didn't Isis tell you that?" she gestured to the picture of Isis.

"Never again."

"Stop it! Stop that! You're just a picture and you can't speak!" She tore the pictures from the door.

"You're just a picture. Nothing more."

She sank back to the floor, a continuous shudder ran through her, cold tingles going down her spine. He was a little behind and beside her, drool dangling from his leering grin. He wasn't there when she turned to look.

"You can't keep bringing him back," she said to the picture. It was wrinkled, the corners torn where it had come away from the pins. She picked it up, smoothed it out and reattached it, doing the same with Isis. Kneeling down, she asked,

"Is he really dead? I killed him. There was hardly any blood. Is he burning in hell?"

"Never again."

"Can't you tell me anything useful?" her voice rose again but she kept her tempter in check. "Can't you tell me he's suffering for what he put me through?"

He was running toward her, eyes glinting in the poor light, fingers clawed, his arm stretched out for her. She yelped, throwing herself to the floor. At any moment she'd feel him tearing at her...

The raven did nothing but stare when she pushed

herself up. Picture or not, she knew it was watching her.

"Never again."

"Get! Get! You are a creature of death. Guidance! You've brought him back so he can kill me."

"Never again."

"Is that all? All you have to say? Will I ever be safe again? I know! Never again." Jo giggled, scrunching herself up when she saw him again, waiting at the end of the hallway, shoulders hunched like they always used to be. She was determined not to fall or hide herself this time, though couldn't help but flinch when he moved toward her. In another instant he was gone and she laughed harder still. He wasn't ever going away and she would always be afraid. The raven returned her stare.

"I'll never be safe. Never again."

Cake & Quill

A Storm Blows Through Polecat County
Donald B. Stephens

Rain fell on the head of Jackson Mallory. The slight mist had turned into a crop-drenching downpour, but Jackson barely noticed. For the last thirty minutes he had stood within spitting distance of the dilapidated shed that sat on the edge of the barnyard, waiting and wishing he didn't have to go inside. It would be dark soon. It was best to get this done before walking back to the house through the puddles formed.

This was by far the hardest thing the eighty-two-year-old widower had ever done. Putting an animal down was never easy, but this was his Jakey. The only dog who was allowed in the house - the only dog he had ever let into his soul.

The whimpers had stopped a few minutes after he had loaded two shells into ole' Betsy and he wondered if there was a way around his predicament.

"Maybe that moron of a city vet is wrong," he mumbled. "Just because he got some learnin 'bout animals, doesn't mean he know everthin. What if Jake's just feelin poorly? No one saw him git bit. I'll bet he caught himself on some barbed-war - caught himself on barbed-war - that's what he did."

The thought seemed to have some merit. His best hunting dog might only have an infection. Jackson didn't trust the new vet, Doctor Jones, who had taken over for old Doc Winters. The man wasn't even as old as his grandson Jimmy - and Jimmy was an idiot. How could a boy, straight out of veterinary school, make such a quick diagnosis without ordering any tests? He couldn't. It had to be a mistake. A coonhound as good as Jake didn't come along every day; it would be a shame to kill an animal for the sake of a misdiagnosis.

"He wanted to put ol' Jakey down right then, just like he were nuttin – like he were one uh muh pigs. Damned city boy. He dern't know a thang 'bout us country foke."

Suddenly, the rain stopped. Jackson looked up and saw a rainbow hanging over dark clouds beyond the dense Kentucky forest. Fading sunlight hit his face. Surely this was a sign that God agreed with Jackson's new theory. He took a step to return to the house to find the number for another vet. Slipping on the wet grass, he stumbled and made a loud splash in a newly formed puddle.

The quiet spring air transformed into a din of ferocious snarling; the likes of which Jackson had never before experienced. He spun around in horror. The entire shed was convulsing, as the horrific howling continued. It looked as though a giant invisible beast was shaking the shelter with its fist. The sights and sounds were like a dagger stabbing away at Jackson's heart. There was no doubt now. Doc Jones was right. He had a rabid dog on his hands.

"Jakey!" Jackson cried out, "Quiet down, boy! It's Pappy, boy. It's Pappy."

In times past, the gentle command would have calmed the dog, but now it only provoked the raging beast into an unnerving guttural howl that sounded more demonic than canine. Sorrow filled Jackson's heart as he steadied himself for the deed. Why was this so difficult? Killing an animal was no more difficult than pointing a gun and pulling the trigger. Even when Jessamine, a Basset Hound who had been his wife Darla's favorite, had taken ill shortly after Darla had passed away,

Jackson did his duty without regret. But this was tearing him up inside. This was going to be hell.

"I must be a gittin soft," he mumbled, as his grip on the shotgun tightened. He crept towards the shed. He was close enough now to see Jake through the crack in the sagging door.

"Oh m' God, Jakey!" he cried. His hand flew up to cover his mouth. "What's happened to you, boy?"

Sorrow gave way to shock as he stared at the seething creature he had left tied to a post inside the shed. The black and tan demon pulling on the leash looked nothing like his beloved hunting dog. Once gentle brown eyes were now filled with malice. His sagging jowls had disappeared into a taunt, menacing grin that was all teeth and foaming saliva. Every muscle on the typically docile hound was stretched tight, drawing ridged lines across his dark coat and making the hair stand on end.

Jackson swallowed hard. Anger welled up inside. Seeing his Jakey transformed into an enraged beast by a mindless disease, made him not only sick to his stomach, but disgusted and furious with his own penny-pinching ways. To think that the best hunting dog this side of Polecat County was about to die by his own hands because he wouldn't spend the few dollars it took to vaccinate his animals for rabies; well, it made him rethink his skepticism of modern medicine. *Maybe those city-slicker vets knew what they were talkin 'bout.*

An iron-willed determination replaced the trepidation that had kept him staring at the shed for half an hour. He simply had to make up for his ignorance and prejudice to set things right. As soon as this thing was done, he would call Doc Jones and have him bring enough vaccine out to protect all the animals on the farm. But right now there was a job to do. Jake had to die.

He reached for the latch and unhooked it. Before the door was fully open, a sharp snap rang out and the seething beast lunged for the opening.

The door slammed into Jackson's chest and knocked him backwards. The ear-splitting explosion of Betsy's wrath filled the air and tore a huge hole in the shed's roof. The old farmer slipped in the mud as he spun around on his knees to face the demon that had forced him to the ground. He still had another barrel and shell ready, which would be more than enough.

Jake was nowhere to be seen.

The blast must a scared 'im into the woods, he thought. The sound of dogs barking changed his mind. "No, Jake!" he cried out, as he stumbled to his feet and started to run, "No! *Stay away from 'em*!"

He rounded the corner of the barn, hoping the chain-link fence to the dog run was stronger than the post that had held Jake in the shed. What he saw made him gasp. Hunter, Molly and Max were barking, biting and pawing furiously at the spot where Jake had pushed up the fence, which had allowed him to get his head onto the cement block of the run. His jaws were snapping at each paw that came within reach. So far it looked as though the other dogs had been quick enough to avoid getting bitten, but Jake was pushing so hard on the fence that Jackson feared he might make his way under it.

Keeping Betsy trained on Jake, Jackson moved to the side of the kennel where any stray buckshot would be sent to the woods instead of hitting one of his prized hunting dogs. He steadied his shaky nerves by leaning against the kennel post. A split-second before he pulled the trigger a flash of lightning and accompanying thunder clap split the air, temporarily blinding him and sending the shot over Jake's head.

Jackson rubbed his eyes and tried to focus through the torrent of rain that was unleashed by the lightning. The dogs were still going crazy, but they had moved to the other side of the kennel. Jake had disappeared again.

Flashes of light, thunderous blasts, howling hounds and gale-force winds filled the barnyard. Through it all Jackson heard the sound of chickens clucking for their lives. Jake was in the coop.

Jackson thought about trying to save his hens, but Betsy was now empty and he had only thought to bring two shells. He wasn't about to face what Jake had become with an empty gun. As fast as his spindly old legs would carry him, he ran back to the house and the box of ammo sitting on the kitchen counter. A handful of shells went into his pocket after two replaced the spent casings that fell onto the floor. He was now ready for the coop.

*****

The door to the small building was flapping in the wind. A lone hen could be heard, crying out at the top of her lungs. A second later it stopped. Flipping the switch to the dim bulb that hung in the center of the coop, Jackson looked upon a scene that made his stomach wretch. Dead and dismembered chickens were strewn about. Blood covered the floor. Feathers danced in the air, blown around by the wind that whipped through the open door.

In the far back corner a dark figure stirred. A low growl accompanied sickening crunching and slurping.

Jackson raised Betsy. Before he could draw a bead on the mad hound, the light flickered and went out. Flashes of lightning illuminated the gory scene like some sort of satanic disco, with the pulsating beat coming from Jackson's heart. His pulse began to race as he watched the fragmented steps of a rabid dog turning to face him.

Jake leaped for his master's throat. Fire erupted from both barrels of the twelve gauge shotgun as Betsy missed her mark yet again, blasting the feeder to shreds.

The blast knocked Jackson off balance and probably saved his life. He stumbled to the left. The hound's blood stained jaws locked onto the barrel of the shotgun instead of his neck.

The angry beast hit him at full speed, knocking them both to the floor with a thud. A sharp pain tore through his side as at least one rib fractured from the fall.

Jake landed on his chest, shaking the gun like he used to do with a stick in a game of take-away. But this was no game. Betsy was now the only barrier between Jackson and death. If Jackson let go of the gun, the soft flesh of his neck would take its place.

The pain was so intense that he feared blacking out. "No!" he screamed, trying to drive the thought from his mind.

Somehow the command got through to the faithful dog that was lying dormant beneath the rage. Jake's countenance softened and he let go of the gun, jumped off his master and sat at his feet. The light came back on. Jackson stared at his dog in disbelief. For a moment, the lovable hound had returned and looked as though he was ready to head out for a hunt.

The shock of all that had happened in such a short time, accompanied by blinding pain and seeing his old friend back in his right mind, was too much for the old farmer. He began to weep. Soft brown eyes stared down at him and beheld him with a curious, playful gaze. Jakey was back.

Treats. Maybe I can give 'im a treat 'ta occupy 'im 'till I crawl outta here. There were dog treats in the same pocket he had stuffed a handful of shotgun shells into. He moved his hand slowly to his pocket. A despair-filled moan escaped his lips. The pocket was empty. Both the shells and the dog biscuits must have fallen from his pocket upon impact with the floor. *They couldn't have gone too far.* He began the frantic search for a cookie, feeling the floor around him, looking as far as the dim-lit room would allow. There – about three yards away – next to a headless hen – the red finger of a shotgun shell and the brown wedge of a dog treat.

Keeping one eye on Jake, he moved towards the treat. The pain was unbearable, but something else made him pause. Each movement seemed to cause a change in his old hunting companion – the beast was coming back.

The bone-chilling growl returned as the demon hound rose to his feet and circled his master.

"No Jake! No!" Jackson yelled. This time, the command had no effect.

Jake moved directly between man and cookie and stopped; as if the disease had given him a greater intelligence and he knew exactly what his master was reaching out to do. He snapped his jowls and pawed at the floor, building up wrath to take out a mortal enemy.

Jackson saw another shell out of the corner of his eye. It was under another hen and only a foot away. He bit his lip and lunged for the shell. At the same time, Jake leapt for his master's throat.

An explosion filled the air. The infuriated hound was thrown to the ground in a bloody heap, right at his master's feet.

"Are you alright?" Martin Jones asked as he dropped the shotgun and rushed to the old farmer's side.

"Muh ribs. I thin I broke muh ribs."

"Oh dear. I'll take you to the hospital. He didn't bite you, did he?"

"Nah. Pert near did, but ya got here just in time, Doc. Just in time."

"Well, I had a feeling you were going to have a hard time with this. It looks like I was right about that too. Next time, let's put down any animal with rabies as soon as we know it – okay?"

"Alright, Doc. Alright."

Damned city vets – always 'ave ta be right. I dread how many times I'm gonna hear, "Trust me. I was right about Jake, and I'm right about this."

We're not in Kansas

James Warren McAllister

I wake in a cold, sweaty shiver.

The nightmare is always the same. Like I have no choice.

I am at the control panel, carefully making the delicate adjustments. To my right, a wall of some transparent material, not quite glass. Behind that, the Survivors.

In front of me is the surgical suite. I have no idea if they called it that, but it's all I can think of.

To my left is another transparent wall, but it seems thicker. *IT* sits there.

Waiting…

I have to concentrate, to do this correctly. I don't have any surgical training, so why it's making me do this, I can't say.

My hands shake. I wipe the sweat from my brow as another shiver ripples through me. I feel light-headed, like I need sugar.

I have to concentrate! A little higher up on the leg… there. I adjust the controls, and the incision is made. I can see the boy's mouth open, but my ears don't hear his screams. But I do…

This is the boy's fourth surgery. It takes only a few minutes to remove his leg. The automation dresses the boy's stump and quickly returns him to the Survivors room as a mechanical arm picks the limb off the table. I can't stop watching it. The toes are twitching.

As the dripping limb moves out of sight, I notice *IT* moving on my left. *IT* is excited, pacing in circles, eyes burning.

The boy's leg appears, still steaming. When *IT* jumps up, the mechanical arm releases the severed flesh. *IT* chomps twice and swallows.

The dream is always the same.

It has been for fifty nights now.

At least, I think they're nights.

I remember everyone on the bus screaming when the dark billows engulfed us.

The next thing I remember is being here.

As bad as the nightmares are, I wish I wouldn't ever wake up. Maybe next time I won't. I can only hope.

They took the biggest ones first. Or, they took one of their arms. Then they put them back, and took another. One about every four hours.

After they'd taken the high school kids' arms, they took the smaller kids.

Whole.

Then they took my left leg.

Then the high school kids' left legs.

Then they took my right leg.

Then they took their right legs.

Then they took my arms, both at once.

Then they took what was left of the kids. Torsos screaming until IT chomped on them.

I look to my left, then my right.

I'm all alone now…

Cryo

Tom Greenwood

He had no idea of the passage of time. That was the problem when you were in cryo; you could have been frozen for ten minutes, ten years, ten millennia or even longer. The last eight times he had been woken up, had not been that long apart, perhaps tens of years at the most. And now he was waking up again.

Would it be his son who woke him? His son who had betrayed him, replaced him, frozen him, woken him six times to taunt him and then on the seventh to ask his advice. Or would it be the two people who had woken him up the last time and claimed his son was dead? Then, they had just put him back into cryo, no arguments, only a statement that they would wake him again in a few years.

Perhaps claiming to be the legal owner of the entire S11 area of the Sphere had been a mistake.

He felt the cryo-coffin change from its horizontal position to vertical, and heat return to his cold bones. The face-partition opened and he looked out into darkness. There was nothing, no light and no sound. Then, after what could only have been five minutes, there was the faint rustle of something moving and some distant clicks and whistles.

"Who's there?" he shouted. "Show yourself."

He was blinded by a bright yellow light. He screwed his eyes up. When he managed to open them again, he saw something move out of the corner of his eye. He tried to focus on it but all he could make out was a green blur.

He grew used to the light, and the whistles and clicks grew louder. From the right came a large green creature with a single eye on top of a stalk. It was dressed in a blue overall. The eye stared at him, and the creature clicked and whistled through a large mouth where its stomach should be.

He closed his eyes and screamed.

He opened them again to see the creature still staring at him. It was standing about two metres away.

Calm, stay calm, there was no reason to assume the alien was dangerous. But then there was no reason to assume that it was friendly either.

The alien looked down at a small device and fiddled with it in its two hands or tentacles or whatever they were. Then a second alien walked or slid beside the first and it too, started whistling, bleeping and clicking. The first one replied. And if he didn't know better, the two seemed to be having an argument. Eventually, the first one handed the device to the second one and walked off, almost as if in a huff. The second alien continued to fiddle with the device. Apparently satisfied, whistled, and then a voice said in Ancient English, "Can you understand me?"

"Yes," he mumbled in reply after a couple of seconds hesitation.

"Are you one of the builders of the Sphere?" the voice asked.

It was probably best to answer truthfully. "My ancestors were. What has happened?"

There was no reply for perhaps thirty seconds. Then a bleep and a whistle sounded and the alien said, "The Xanwiths found the Sphere drifting between galaxies surrounding a dying star. It was too valuable to allow them to have it, so we declared a holy war. It is the most marvellous ancient construct we have ever found that was possibly built by the ancient race only known as the Ancients. Though we cannot be sure it was them, as all signs of the builders had been erased by time. Until we found you."

"How long?"

"So you are an Ancient?"

He would have shrugged his shoulders if he had been able to. "I suppose I might be. What did they look like?"

The alien started a heated, annoyingly untranslated debate with what he could only assume was the other one which remained out of sight.

"What is wrong?" he asked.

"There is nothing wrong," it replied.

He knew when he was being lied to, even by a one-eyed, green alien.

"How long have I been in cryo?" he asked again.

"We think about 50 thousand million zaltons."

That sounded a long time. "How long is a zalton?"

"Twenty-eight sarons."

Well, that was a great help, he thought.

"Are any other of the cryo-caskets occupied?" he asked.

"No, they are all broken. Yours was the only one still functioning. In fact it is the only piece of equipment we have found that is still functioning on the millions and millions of zandons of the Sphere."

The eye blinked.

"Why were you in the suspended animation machine?" the alien asked. "We have found remains of them in other places, but never one occupied."

"I was placed here by my son." His son who had betrayed him.

"Your son? Why was that?"

He closed his eyes for a couple of moments to collect his thoughts. It was probably best to tell only a partial truth. "He grew jealous and wanted everything I had." He stopped; it was probably best to change the subject. Declaring yourself absolute ruler and starting your own religion with yourself as a deity would probably be frowned upon by most species and therefore probably by these aliens too. "How are you speaking to me? How did you learn the ancient language?"

"A universal translator. It has many unknown languages programmed into it. We guessed this one might be yours. It is an ancient device first created by the Piloths from quadrant four of the third galaxy. They were great archaeologists. Then when the Farinoiths declared war the Piloths fought …"

He stopped listening; he was the last human alive. If what the aliens were saying was true, he had been in cryo for millions of years and if the red dwarf star surrounded by the Sphere was nearing the end of its life, then it was more like thousands of millions of years. Had he slept longer than the age the universe had been when he had originally been alive? He started to sweat at the implication.

His thoughts were interrupted by the alien whistling, bleeping and thumping the universal translator.

"That's better. Bleep whistle Piloths!"

"And there are no other beings like me?" he asked.

"None at all. There are legends, legends of a mighty race that spanned the five known galaxies; a race that grew decadent and fell under the sway of a single being who declared himself Lord. His progeny grew weary of this and led a rebellion and then he declared himself Lord. Lord of all creation, and insisted that all bow down before him. This led to a war, a mighty war that all but destroyed the Ancients. But then these are just legends, legends of the evil race of the Ancients, used to scare children when they won't behave."

That sounded a bit like people. Parts of it almost

reflected his own life.

"But now we have found one. A member of the race of the evil Ancients."

"What are you going to do with me?"

"We don't know. There is only you. So not enough of you to keep as a subject race. Can your species replicate … No you don't look as if you could. We may trade you to the Jajains; they like to experiment, and they will copy your genetic material. Or we may keep you alive, but the resource wars mean you are not important except as a curiosity. We …"

He was alone. He was the last human alive. If he was lucky he would be kept as a curiosity for aliens; if he was unlucky, then … Best not think about it.

"… the thirty-five clans of the Verinols will pay a great price for a living Ancient. Though we would need to prove that you really are an Ancient and not some monstrosity created in some genetic laboratory."

The alien was interrupted by a sound.

The sound of laughter.

Human laughter.

Then a vaguely familiar voice said, "Sorry, I couldn't keep a straight face any longer. Twenty-eight sarons, I nearly lost it then – ha ha ha."

Then someone else started laughing and the alien just disappeared in a flash of holographic light. From the left, two people approached.

It was the two people who had claimed his son was dead.

The Agony of Defeat
James Warren McAllister

The whistle blew, ending the chaos. I looked up at the clock, trying to avoid the score emblazoned there. Three, two, one. Suddenly I felt tired, old, sore. I let out a deep breath I didn't remember taking in.

47 to 44. Losing was not good. My eyes followed the team, bloodied and bruised, slogging off the field. Three games in a row. One more and there will be a new Captain for sure. Maybe even today.

I followed them into the dressing room. It didn't take long for the small space to fill with the stench of sweat, blood, and dirt. The team mulled about, letting the loss drip off them with their sweat. Down, defeated, beaten.

Dead.

"Good effort, men. But we need more. We have the tools to win the next game. We will hone them in two days. Practice Wednesday at 9:00AM sharp."

My voice was as pitiful, but sounded better than I had thought it would. I limped stiffly to my cubicle and glanced at the whirlpool. The line was long.

Damn.

I sat on the bench. After a time of studying my cleats, I pulled the jersey and shoulder pads over my head as a unit. The cold air hit my drenched tee shirt as the jersey steamed at my feet. A strong odor like garlic and vanilla told me not to look up. The bench moved, so I turned to look at the feet of whoever sat next to me.

"Aille m'scrundlat, hgsta frengol whet-wet. Tellna

d'rec mortin waster fin."

"Do you want to remove me now, Master?"

"Norint. Aille m'scrundlat grelaelt. Hastre…"

"Thank you, Master." All emotion drained from me. "Which ones?"

"Anderson, McCauliffe, aaehr… Simon."

Only three. The Skorlt who owned us got off with a light sentence. That meant we did, too.

"Yes, Master. When will the replacements arrive?"

"Scralpt! Wesstellam melt rik jaustein!"

"Sorry, Master."

The Skorlt left. I reached into my cubby and pulled out the knife and the mat. I placed the mat on the floor.

"Anderson! McCauliffe! Simon!"

The three nervously came forward. I pointed to the mat with the knife. Simon glanced at the Skorlt guards by the door, then joined the other two in assuming the position. Hands and knees on the mat, head bent forward, forehead touching the mat.

The rest of the team kept their backs to us. I was thankful for that.

Simon was shaking, so I went to him first. I placed the tip of the knife on the back of his neck where it joined his head, angled towards the top of it.

They tell me you don't feel a thing this way.

Only the dead slaves really know.

Sea Of Contradictions

William Douglas Frank

Shrieking infants in my head.
I have fallen, yet I ain't dead.
Burning alive in my own bed.
Grieving for the woman who bears my dread.
Screaming, crying, falling without motion!
Pleading, grieving, weeping forth an ocean!
Dancing through your joy, yet lacking all emotion!
So, come on darling, bring me my end!
Bring it sweetheart, a soul must shed its skin!
Every breath spent.
Surviving this personality that cannot pretend.
Sea of contradictions.
Please just make it end.
Harbinger of nothingness, bless me with control!
Deadly living, tear me apart and make me whole.
The agonies of lifelessness burrow through my feckless soul.
Fury through weeping, heat through the snow!
This sea of contradictions makes life so very dull!
So, come on baby, slice me whole!
Burning and freezing!
Dying yet breathing!
My hands extend from the void quivering amidst the horrors of your dreaming!
Kill me, caress me, torture me, protect me!
Curse me, praise me, silence me, detain me!
Do what you need.

Just drown this sea of contradictions that has enveloped my being!
A thousand thoughts racing!
Identity fleeting!
Sea of contradictions.
I beg for your believing!
The chaos never ends as long as I am breathing.
Cackling through your weeping!
Dry as I am bleeding.
Eternally awake.
I know I am dreaming.

Hippopotomonstrosesquipedaliophobia
Adam Oster

Oh God, oh God, oh God, oh God. What alternative do I possibly have available for my next course of action? I am now only two cycles of the hour hand away from my deadline and absolutely no closer to a completed correction than when I had begun this non-viable assignment. I am in the precise situation as the one I had found myself when I was originally commissioned with this insurmountable undertaking a mere ten hours earlier.

What had been coursing through my mind at that time to allow me to become the patsy? I could have simply made my egress from the complex at the moment I had been directed to present myself within Mr. Forebald's office. Flight would have been the more appropriate path for me to have taken, knowing he is not one prone to deliver pleasant news at the conclusion of the workday. If I had abdicated, I would have never known how red his square visage could be as he shrieked his infamous, "What the hell is this?" at me, all the while flailing my dissertation above his head as though it were nothing more than a selection of waste paper.

Immediately upon entering his suite, his inability to recognize the impressive collection of data regarding a revolutionary new turn in anti-anxiety medication was apparent. Unfortunately, even at this moment, I had not the foresight to remove myself from his presence.

I had dedicated a full week of my occupational life,

as well as a great deal of my personal, toward establishing the pristine accuracy of this document, which, I might add, had been requested for me to piece together to ensure further funding for our keystone development.

This knowledge did not appear to faze the large man who, unfortunately, currently holds a position of power over me, and so I was left to stand inside the doorway of his workspace and stare, dumbfounded in how to respond to such a harsh greeting.

"Get the hell in here, Schmertz, and tell me what the hell you think you're doing trying to submit this bullshit. I don't know what you boys down in R&D think you're getting away with here, but I'm sure as hell not going to stand for it."

I had entered the room slowly and allowed myself to sit within the low-set chair directly in front of his imposing desk. He had glared down his nose at me, a method he overtly utilized in order to remain at his most imposing, whilst setting me at unease.

"Well?" he had growled. I remember an unfamiliar anger had begun to well up within me at that utterance. It was as if some primal entity within me felt it needed to lash out at this man who held my destiny within his hands. The voice of that entity was easily quelled upon the recognition of his power.

"I apologize, sir, however, I cannot be certain what might have caused you to develop such an unhappy attitude toward me. I believe I created my thesis in a manner which should be considered as articulate and exhaustive as could be expected, which was something of a Herculean task, I might add, due to—"

"There you go again," he interjected whilst baring his teeth at me in his frustration. Again the primal monster within me cried to be allowed its escape. Again, I fought against its call, knowing it held no power in opposing the demon in front of me.

"Sir?"

"Making up words. Those damned long words of yours that you just make up in order to hide the truth."

"Sir? If you're stating that my phrasing is disproportionate with your expectat—"

"Quit it!" he had screamed as he stood and pointed toward the door. "I want none of that in here! Get out there, fix this report," he had said as he thrust the crumpled pile of papers into my face," and get it to me before my 6am meeting tomorrow morning."

"But, sir—"

"No buts. If I don't have a way of showing my bosses that you're actually doing something down there in your creepy lab by tomorrow morning, they're going to shut it all down. Do you understand me? Shut. It. Down. That means no job for you, and more importantly, no job for me. There's a lot riding on this, so make it simple, make it short, and make it quick. Got me?"

"Yes, sir," I had replied after a brief pause. "Yes. I get you." I had continued stammering stupidly as I exited his office. The monster within me had completely disappeared, apparently deciding there must be other methods to feed its frenzy than within my pathetic frame. At its departure, I found my vocabulary had also deserted me.

So, there I had been, utterly confused by exactly what Mr. Forebald had found to be at fault within the document, yet left to be the individual who would enact the necessary changes which might appropriate his happiness. I stared at the papers as I stood in front of the elevator awaiting its arrival.

I still can't believe he had accused me of making up words. The man has red lines all over these pages, striking out words like alprazolam and abdominal, and multiple lines being used to strike out each usage of the word lightheadedness.

As the head of a pharmaceutical laboratory, the man must certainly understand such a simple word as lightheadedness, should he not?

Braedon Forebald, the red-faced, square-headed gentleman, and I utilize the word loosely, had been only recently transferred to become the supervisory manager of our laboratory. I'm mostly unfamiliar with the man, outside of the rumors of how incredibly demanding he is and how those demands generally revolve around questionable reasons. The conversation I had with him earlier today would easily support that summation.

God, what could I possibly do? He claims this document holds the fate of our entire research and development laboratory in its hands, while also declaring it does not pass his obviously inscrutable muster. How could this possibly be anything but the absolutely most beautiful piece of scientific prose anyone working within pharmaceuticals today has laid their eyes upon? It is nothing short of immaculate.

I'm going to get fired. I'm going to get everyone fired. There's no fancy way of saying it, no simple way of avoiding it. I will be the cause of the summary termination of every single employee I ever considered a friend. And why? Simply because I am not able to understand the whims of a raging maniac?

What could he possibly expect from all of this? I don't know the man well, perhaps I misunderstood him. In fact, that conversation, the one where he demanded I rewrite one of the most demanding pieces of literature I have ever composed, was easily the longest discussion we have ever had. Considering that, it should be easy to understand that his expectations of me here are appreciably incomprehensible. The man intends for me to telepathically determine his intentions behind these simplistic markings.

The only thought I have toward what might have caused him to become so profusely angered is that he, for some peculiar reason, has had a falling out with words that stretch on longer than five letters. This is a rather dangerous predicament for a man who currently holds an R&D division of a pharmaceutical laboratory under his charge.

Pharmaceutical laboratory could possibly be considered too extended a phrase for a man of his particular ailment. Perhaps we should be required to re-christen it simply as The Lab. Or perhaps the Drug-Makey Place?

Dammit! If only I hadn't been so damned confident and individualized my distress. Hiro would have been the perfect assistant for this gargantuan task. It's not as though I didn't have the opportunity to request his assistance. In fact, as the elevator doors had opened to take me from Mr. Forebald's floor and return to the one in which I find myself most comfortable, who had I been lucky enough to find but Hiro himself. Obviously, he had been waiting for me, seeking to determine the purpose for my being called to the Twenty-third floor to meet with management.

He had held a cautious appearance at my arrival, which immediately morphed into one of intense apprehension as he noticed my own composure.

"Didn't go well, huh?" Hiro had asked. Hiro is tall, lanky, and completely awkward, but somehow he is able to utilize all of these character descriptions, which many would consider faults, into a certain sense of charm. In fact, although he's an amazingly ungainly individual, he also happens to be the most extroverted laboratory technician of the lot of us.

I really like Hiro. He has always managed to assist me in escaping my interpersonal shell when I would much rather be located deep inside, perhaps reading an unfamiliar equipment manual, as opposed to developing small talk for use with unknown people.

It is thanks to him that my response to his question was a simple pointing of a singular phalanx toward my temple and a cocking of the thumb before firing it forward.

"Damn," Hiro had frowned as he pressed the button for the fourteenth floor. "So, what does that mean for darts tonight?"

"I couldn't possibly have any opportunity for engaging in social activities with you this evening, Hiro. Mr. Forebald has tasked me with the impossible project of completely revising the—"

"Sheesh, Walt, buddy. Cool it with the over-explanation. A simple no would suffice, you know?"

"I apologize."

"So, you've gotta rewrite the paper? That's lame."

"Super-lame," I had said. I have long feared the usage of vernacular, simply due to how graceless it feels as it falls from my lips. However, Hiro insists upon it, so I attempt to emulate his speech patterns whenever I am discussing with him, as I know he will not reply with laughter, but with advice, should my attempts at utilizing it go awry.

"So, what was the problem? Did he catch the joke I hid within the chemical equation for our beta blocker solution?"

Even in my terrible mood, I was unable to keep from laughing at the idea.

"What? Was it that? Because if it is, I can definitely rework the equation in a matter of minutes. I have the real one just down at my desk actually. I've felt terrible about the whole thing—"

"It's not that, Hiro. He merely suggested that I may have overcomplicated the explanation of our product and requested I redevelop the document to meet something of a less-scientifically-minded audience's requirements."

"So, not nerds, huh?"

"Precisely."

"Okay, well, that kinda sucks, but it's not that hard to do, is it? I mean, if you want, I can help you with it and we can get it knocked out in an hour or two."

"I couldn't possibly expect you to relinquish your evening for me, Hiro. If I'm not mistaken, tonight is the night when you had intended to seek out that bartender you have been harboring feelings toward. I don't believe I—"

"Dude, I can do that any night. I mean, we only see her like every other day now."

"Don't fret yourself regarding my current situation," I had replied as the elevator doors opened to the fourteenth floor, where the R&D labs reside. "I'll put in place the requisite corrections and make my way out into the world and on the search for you before you're even aware of my absence."

"Alright, pal. But just so you know, I speak the language of the people. Might help to have someone like me around, you know, being bilingual and all that."

"I'll contact you via text message if your knowledge of the vernacular could become of any use to me."

"Perfect," Hiro had smiled as the elevator doors closed between us.

In retrospect, the decision to reject Hiro's offer of assistance could have been an even worse decision than the one to not attempt to disappear from the building prematurely. He is the obvious choice in someone who would be able to clear up my language. He can be rather difficult to work with on tedious tasks such as this, especially with a decreased timeline and an opportunity for social interaction at the ready; however, he is also the only person I know who could possibly understand the inner workings of a man like Forebald. At the time of

Hiro's heroic offering of assistance, I could only envision him standing over my shoulders, hopping in his eagerness to depart the building. Now, all I can think about is how stupid I had been.

The entire fate of the lab hinges on this assignment and for the first time in my life, I had decided to allow my confidence to take over and suggest that I required no assistance in completing the task.

I glance down at the second page and note the six question marks surrounding the word hippocampus.

I'm going to get fired. Hiro's going to be fired. My entire department is going to get fired. Simply because I couldn't ask for help.

Perhaps he'd still be willing to help. Two hours is more than enough time for someone like Hiro to make this legible for a kindergartner. Of course, at this hour, he's either nursing a nasty hangover or that bartender he had been hoping to take home.

I place the papers on my desk in frustration, causing the screen to light up due to the movement of the computer's mouse. A loud sigh escapes my lips, which, under normal circumstances, would have brought Hiro over immediately in order to provide some sort of comic relief.

However, there's no one else here. There hasn't been anyone for hours. It's four a.m. on a Thursday. No one in their right mind would be here at this hour. Unless, of course, they had been tasked with crafting the salvation for this entire department.

I lean back in my chair and pull the papers toward me, looking more directly at the information held within. The first item I notice is how they have been placed out of order. I rearrange the fifteen pages to their proper pagination and peruse the opening for the first of the plethora of notes from Mr. Forebald. It doesn't take long, as he had already found reason to produce marks to the page by the very first words I had submitted. A line of red struck all the way through the title of my paper with what I'm fairly certain are the words "What the hell?!?!!!!" written beside it. Those words themselves are underlined countless times.

"Seems like as good of a place as any to start," I say out loud to myself, feeling my heart palpitate at the very idea of beginning this all again.

When I had been at this moment ten hours ago, I hadn't seen my situation as being quite so dire as I do right now. I had certainly felt the immense pressure regarding my completion of these rectifications. Yet, Mr. Forebald had managed to give me something of an amazing challenge. A puzzle. One that would require an inordinate amount of brainpower to overcome. Here I was, a man whose vocabulary knew no bounds, needing to develop boundaries for the words which wished to escape the confines of my vast intellectual prowess.

A dime's worth of hours later and my eagerness to solve this puzzling dilemma is much less available.

No time to consider the past any longer. I must focus on the task at hand, keep to the moment. Although not a single word is changed from the ones I began with, the expectations are still the same. As well as the possible outcome, should I fail in my task.

I crack my fingers and set myself back to work. Perhaps I simply need to think about all of this in a completely different manner. The first few times I approached the work, I had utilized the idea of cutting and trimming out some of the more explanatory pieces that could be considered superfluous. Perhaps what was truly needed was a translation. The current title is Selective Serotonin Reuptake Inhibitors to be Used in Conjunction with Benzodiazepines.

To be completely honest, I'm not quite certain how this title could be any further concise. Obviously, this is the basic premise of the medication we have been developing, to utilize a long term solution with a short term one. Perhaps his question here was whether or not I would be able to make this title punchier, to give it some of that pizazz which Hiro always speaks of? I'm not entirely certain how many buzzwords apply to SSRIs. Even if there were, would I really wish to dilute the subject matter of my publication purely for sensationalism?

And what if this wasn't the purpose behind Mr. Forebald's decision to highlight my thesis statement and include his ever-so-descriptive question of what it was? I could put effort into this momentous definition of what my paper was to express only to find that it wasn't what he wished to have me correct. And if I were to go about my corrections following an entirely inappropriate line of thinking, it could cause even further backlash, and even further danger for my division.

Perhaps I should have directed myself back to his office the first time I had reviewed these notes and requested further explanation of what precisely he was looking for when he placed these pieces of paper within my hands.

After pondering that possible course of action for several moments, I'm reminded of how he had responded to my initial requests for clarification. It would have appeared that Mr. Forebald is not a man who feels the need to explain himself. Or express himself without a great deal of aggression.

Perhaps he could make use of some of our Benzodiazepines.

I finally make the decision to include both possible interpretations of his question in my rewriting of the heading. How a Long-Term Solution and a Short-Term Solution can be Used to Create a Full Solution. It takes me over ten minutes to get to this version of my title, finding it difficult to allow myself to keep from using a direct reference to either type of medication we began our research with.

I stare at the screen and suddenly become aware of one final issue. The word solution is well above what I assume is Mr. Forebald's five character limit on words. I search my mental thesaurus for possible synonymous alternatives: Answer, Resolution, and even Panacea, but all seem to be too far and away from what Mr. Forebald would be willing to accept.

Fix!

How we Can Fix a Big Thing with Two Things.

The most atrocious sentence I have ever written, or even considered writing. But there it is, on the page, for me to place all of the work I had performed these past few months beneath.

I feel tears well up within the corners of my eyes. I can't do this. There is no possible way I could be able to perform the necessary corrections to meet my manager's needs. Mr. Forebald wishes for me to do the impossible, to make a publication which required the use of severely long and technical terms, into something that a child could comprehend.

That entity rises within me again. I feel a fog roll in across my mind, a part of myself shutting off against me.

Perhaps this wasn't the most important thing I have ever completed, but it's good. I'm proud of it. And this charlatan wishes for me to murder it through the extreme slaughter of word, grammar, precision of language, and, most painful of all, simplicity.

Chemical engineering is not simple, it's perfection, yet this bear of a man wishes to make it into something just anyone could approach as though they were experts. I recognize the situation in that we are operating on an ever-decreasing budget, but to think that I could ever compromise my own integrity, merely to provide something to the stock holders which they can glom onto with their idiotic minds, well, that's purely...

It could never work. We're all doomed! Even within my standard conversations, I don't believe I could limit myself to such a small number of characters to a given locution. Expression is nothing without precision, and precision simply cannot exist without utilizing the appropriate vocables. To put it in terms Mr. Forebald could understand: I simply do not possess the talents to complete this goal.

That could possibly be a bit too convoluted of a sentence for his sentiments.

Perhaps, instead, it would make more sense for me to state it like this: This stuff was too hard for me to do.

I suddenly become aware that I've gone through this all before. Several times. In my absolute terror of performing poorly in my given task, I've managed to cycle through the same madness time and again, wasting hours of my life for, what?

Back to work.

First sentence. The one in which I managed to, what I would claim to be rather concisely, state the basic thesis behind all of our work, the concept that directed us forward from the first moment we were developed into a research faction and led our every thought as we considered our development of our miracle cure.

I only make it halfway through the reading of that first sentence before I completely break down into tears. I push myself away from my desk, allowing my movable seating apparatus to come to a quick stop on the textured floor beneath me before I stand in a fit of rage and begin pacing.

"This is impossible!" I shout into the empty room. I hear my voice echo through the white halls and cubicles that are my current surroundings. The white noise machine had been turned off hours ago, causing this floor to feel even emptier than it usually would.

For the record, I would like to state that the sound which is produced by such appliances is not actually white noise, but pink, or, I suppose there are several other colors of the sound spectrum it could be, but definitely not white.

However, I digress.

I am now nothing less than completely frozen with trepidation revolving around the possible outcomes of this evening's production, or lack thereof, before I finally become aware that I have been staring at the screen for almost another hour. I now have less than thirty minutes before Mr. Forebald will be expecting a completed work and I have nothing more than a terrible correction to the title of the document. A correction which I have already modified back to its original form several times.

Perhaps I could simply cram together a few sentences that would give the basic understanding of the magic we had performed up here on the 14th floor, thereby risking not only my integrity, but also my job when the stockholders receive a R&D document which feels as though it were written by a twelve-year-old.

Who am I kidding? I would require at least another twelve hours to complete such a document. And a team of scientists. If I could perform a duty as that, I would have been outside this building hours ago enjoying a series of recreational activities with my favorite acquaintances.

Of course, there is the consideration that the only person in any true danger here is myself. Surely, the men that Mr. Forebald is intending to present this document to have seen similar works in the past, as I have submitted many over the time of my employment. The only new variable within this equation is Mr. Forebald himself.

He would not be happy, should I present him with the same precise documents he had given me to destroy, but I believe in the work I had done, and I'm certain any other person within the pharmaceutical industry worth their position would recognize it as well, meaning, the R&D division should be safe, especially considering how important it is toward the continued growth of our company.

It is I who would face the chopping block.

God, how I wish I did not need to consider the needs of the many here. An apartment is just about to open up on the north side of town which I had been hoping to place a deposit on. This idea could not possibly be within my best interests should my occupation be on the line.

However, the path is obvious, even if it is the path of most personal disaster.

I click upon the print button on my screen in order to get a new version of precisely the same document which had been returned to me on the previous evening.

Trepidatiously, I make my way toward the elevator after retrieving my stack of papers from the printer, placing a clip on them as the doors open and I press the button for the 23rd floor.

I feel my heart pound in my chest as the elevator ascends. The papers in my hands quiver at my own trembling. Although I know this is the appropriate decision, it is not any easier to place a nail within the lid of my own coffin. I might as well be tendering my resignation with this act. But I must face the fear, or risk everything.

The elevator doors open again and I am greeted with a very different sight than what I had expected.

Blood covers the walls and desks. And as the centerpiece of the display I see the same man I had spent my sleepless night fearing, strung up upon the whiteboard on the far wall, his chest cavity opened and the innards pulled out into a neat pile on the desk below him.

My jaw falls in terror as the doors again close due to my inactivity.

A voice appears within the constraints of my mind. A cackling voice. One that seems pleased. One that seems satisfied. A heavy burden suddenly feels lifted off my shoulders.

Yet, I cannot help but consider that today might be a perfect one to phone in ill.

Cake & Quill

Late

Angelika Rust

Three o' clock. Time I got off my PC.
You'll be home soon.
I stretch, and switch off the screen.
You'll be hungry when you get home.
I stand and make my way to the kitchen. Five past three.
You'll already be on your way.
I root through the fruit basket. An apple, maybe? A banana? I decide on the apple. You may be a little late. If I peel and cut the banana now, it will be brown by the time you arrive, and you won't like it.
I cut the apple in neat little quarters, remove the core and put the pieces on a plate. Ten past three.
You'll be here any moment now.
I go to the living room and leave the plate on the table, then go back to the kitchen to add a glass of water. You never drink enough. I always give you a bottle of water in the morning, to drink throughout the day. You always bring it back home still full.
Fifteen past three. Looks like you're dawdling again. I told you not to do that. I told you Mommy would get worried.
I look out the kitchen window. A neighbor passes by, sees me and waves. No sign of you. I frown.
Back to the living room. I sit down at the table. Today's newspaper lies open next to my empty coffee mug. I skim a few pages. Twenty past three.

Where are you?

Back to the kitchen. Another glance out the window. Maybe I'll just make myself another coffee. Maybe you forgot something at school and had to go back. Surely you'll arrive any second now.

Twenty-five past three. I'm pacing now. What could possibly take you so long? You've never been that late before. The apple is turning brown. I'll have to eat it myself if you don't come home soon.

Kitchen again. The sidewalk is empty.

Half past three. I throw on my jacket and step into my shoes, wasting time with fumbling for the laces, wasting more time with hunting for my keys.

Outside. I run. All the way to school and back. And again. Where are you? I told you not to talk to strangers. I told you not to take offered sweets. I told you not to go with them, no matter what they say. Not if they just want to show you something. Not if they want to drive you home, because it's cold and raining, and really, you'd be safe and warm in the car. Not even if they told you Mommy had an accident and they were asked to drive you to the hospital. I told you I wouldn't send a stranger in such a case. I told you it would all be a lie.

I search every possible route from school to home and back again. Where can you possibly be?

There's nothing I can do but go back home. Maybe I missed you and you're already there, waiting for me, confused that there's nobody to open the door.

You're not waiting for me.

The front yard is empty.

As is the house.

The apple is brown.

What do I do now?

Phone the police? What would be the use? They don't get active unless a person is missing for more than 24 hours, or do they? Maybe that's just a rumor. It has to be.

What do I do?
>   Just call them.
>   I reach for the phone.
>   There's a missed call.
>   Number suppressed.

Cake & Quill

The Beginning of the End
Rubianne Wood

Somewhere, deep in the darkness, he could hear the soft, tortured cry, the whimpering of a small child, the moaning of a woman in pain. He couldn't remember anything; not where he was or how he had entered this darkness. He found he was injured. His leg ached and he couldn't stand on it. Under his fingers, he could feel a smooth, cool surface – not concrete, perhaps a tiled floor.

He shouted out to anyone who would answer. "Who is here?"

"I am," a small voice said near him. "I am here, John. I think I am hurt, though."

It was his girlfriend, Stacy. Now he could vaguely remember going out. Where? They had wanted to go to dinner and perhaps the park later.

"Stacy, where are we?" he asked with a tremor in his voice.

"I think we are under the restaurant or something. We were eating. Then everything exploded. John, I'm scared. I can't see anything. Am I blind or is it really totally dark?"

He groped around to find her. His hand touched something soft. "Is this you?"

"Yes," she said and grasped his hand with her own.

"I think it is totally dark, I can't see anything, either," he told her, squeezing her hand gently. "Do you think you can stand?"

"Yes," she said and let go of his hand. He heard her moan as she stood. "I can stand, but I think my arm is broken. It feels wet. I think I'm bleeding."

Suddenly he remembered that his cell phone was in his pocket. It wouldn't be a lot of light, but better than none. He pulled it out and flipped it open. He could make out Stacy standing beside him. He moved the light upwards. She was bleeding from a long cut on her lower arm. He couldn't see her face, but he heard her shocked gasp.

He shone the light down to his leg. He couldn't detect any injury through the fabric of his blue jeans. It still hurt. "I think my leg is broken, too. Do you think you can help me to stand?"

"I can help you, son," came a male voice a few feet away. "I don't know how, but I seem to be okay." A flashlight switched on, blinding them momentarily. "My name's Jack. I'm security at the hotel. I'm going to go look for help. You stay here. Try to call for help on that cell phone. We need to see if we can get everyone still alive out of here."

Jack saw Stacy's arm and, without asking, stripped her sweater off of her and wrapped it tightly around her bleeding wound.

"Owe!" she cried out.

"Sorry, ma'am. It's gotta be tight." He flashed his light over John. "Sir, it might be best for you to stay seated until I can get help. You don't want to damage that leg more. I'll be back soon."

John felt a little better knowing Jack was there. He could see his flash light move throughout the space, stopping occasionally to help and reassure someone.

He remembered that he was supposed to be calling for help and dialed 911. All he got was a busy signal. He tried to call his mother, but got the same.

"Stacy, do you have your phone with you?" he asked.

"I did. It was in my purse, but I have no idea where it is now." She sighed deeply. "My arm is really starting to hurt bad, John."

"Just hold on, honey. Jack seems to know what he is doing."

Stacy sat back down beside him. He pulled her against his side for comfort. "There are dead people all around us, I think," she said, "I saw them when Jack flashed his light around."

John had noticed, too, but hadn't wanted to mention it. "Whatever happened is really bad. Must have been a bomb or something. I think we might be in the basement of the hotel. The restaurant is on the ground floor," he told her. "I hope Jack can find a way out."

He tried calling 911 over and over, but without success. The cries and moans were getting quieter. He hoped that didn't mean more people were dying.

"You want to try your mom?" he asked, handing Stacy the phone.

She got no answer either and began to cry, her head on his shoulder.

Suddenly, a bright flash appeared before John's eyes. It was another explosion, and this one was the end.

*****

John woke up drenched in sweat. He sat up, grabbed the water glass on the bedside table and downed what was left in it. He looked through the pile of dirty clothes on the floor and picked out the cleanest from the lot, then went to the small bathroom.

This was his third dream of this sort, he thought as he stepped into the shower. He didn't even know a girl named Stacy. She had been in every one of his dreams, together with some huge disaster. In the first one, they had been trapped in a burning building, the second, a car accident, but this one really was the grand prize winner for nightmare of the year. If this Stacy ever showed up in real life, he would run the other way!

And who was this Jack? He was the would-be hero in each dream, yet he never managed to save them. He and Stacy died every time. It all seemed so real, as if it was actually happening. There was none of the foggy vagueness that usually blurred his memory of dreams.

John dressed for work, though it was several hours too early. There was no point in trying to get back to sleep. He went into his living-room and turned on the television, needing the comfort of the background noise. Only people who lived alone felt the need to have the TV on continually, whether they were watching or not. There was something sinister about a quiet house.

He went to his tiny kitchen and started some coffee. He brushed the week old box of donuts to the side of the table and sat down to wait.

Stacy sure was a looker, he thought looking aimlessly at the wall in front of him. Why was it that he couldn't keep a girl? He wasn't bad looking himself. At twenty-six years old, he was still in his prime. He wasn't the hunk of the year by any means, but he had nice wavy hair and large brown eyes. Didn't chicks like brown eyes anymore? He unconsciously stroked his beard. Maybe it was the facial hair. Well, too bad! He had worked far too long to grow it and he wasn't about to shave it now for some doomsday girl named Stacy!

He got up and poured himself a cup of coffee. Deciding to forego the milk and sugar, he took a drink of the strong black brew. He looked around his kitchen and realized that it had been a while since he had cleaned it. There were three pizza boxes stacked on the counter next to a sink overflowing with dirty dishes. Geez! He was going to have to start buying paper plates, he thought as he started to clean up the trash.

By the time he needed to leave for work, he had gotten the kitchen sparkling clean and even mopped the floor. Maybe the nightmare served a purpose after all. He nodded approvingly as he stepped out the door, and was even whistling when he descended the stairs to leave the building.

*****

The rest of the week was uneventful. No more dreams, at least. It wasn't until the next Monday that it happened. John was in the supermarket, minding his own business, when a familiar figure appeared at the end of the cereal aisle.

He glanced over at the woman and instantly recognized her. He turned away quickly before she could see him, and held a box of Captain Crunch in front of his face. Pretending to be reading the ingredients, he stood frozen in place until she moved past him toward the check-out. He turned cautiously and could see her from the back, standing in line. It was Stacy. There was absolutely no doubt.

Panicking, John threw down the box of cereal, left his grocery cart, full of food, and ran for the door. He quickly made it to the parking lot and searched for his car. In his state of mind, he couldn't remember where he parked it. Oh, God! He had to get out of here now!

He breathed a sigh of relief as a truck pulled out of a nearby space and revealed his car in the next spot. He began a brisk walk when he heard the voice behind him.

"Sir, sir! You dropped your phone!" Great! It was Stacy's voice. Well, he would just have to get a new phone, he thought as he climbed into his car and sped off as if the devil were on his tail. He drove straight home, checking his rear view mirror every few seconds to make sure she wasn't following him.

*****

John paced back and forth through the living-room, trying to comprehend what was happening. He had dreamed the girl and there she was, bright as brass. She had the same red, shoulder length hair, flashing green eyes and lily white skin. How could it be? Could he have met her somewhere before and incorporated her into his dreams?

He took a deep breath and began to calm down a bit. That surely was the case. He must have seen her somewhere before. Perhaps he had gone to school with her, or maybe she worked in a place he frequented. Even as he was reassuring himself, he knew in his heart that it wasn't true. He had never met her, or he would have remembered. A face like hers was not easily forgotten.

John flopped down on the couch and forced himself to relax. It was working. Not only was he emotionally exhausted, but he had had a long day of lifting crates and his body was ready to give out. He had almost dozed off when the phone rang. It startled him and he jumped from the couch at the shrill noise.

He let it ring a couple of times. What if it was her? His home number was on his cell phone. But then again, what if it was Bill from work? He had to answer it.

He picked up on the forth ring. "Hello?"

"Johnny! Are you okay? You sound upset," the woman said, sounding concerned.

"No, Mom. I'm fine," John said, relieved once again.

"Well, you could call once in a while. I get worried." She paused a moment. "Are you keeping your laundry up? I noticed that you haven't been by in a couple of weeks to do it."

"Yeah, Ma. Hey, I'm sorry. I should have come to check on you. Are you okay? Do you need anything?" John was really ashamed of himself.

"I'm fine, sweetheart. Just missing my boy! I got worried when that girl called earlier. She said she found your cell phone. I hope it's okay. I gave her your address. She wanted to return it."

John was stunned, speechless. She had given Stacy his address?

"John, are you there, honey?"

"Uh, yeah, Mom. It's okay. I'll come by tomorrow to see you. I love you." John couldn't keep the tremor out of his voice.

"All right, sweetie. I'll see you tomorrow. Come for dinner."

John heard the click as his mother hung up. Then he silently put the phone in the cradle. God, God, God! Stacy had his address and was coming here to return the phone. What should he do now?

He ran to the front door and made sure it was locked and bolted. Then he went to take a shower, hoping she would come while he was in there and he wouldn't hear the buzzer.

There was no such luck. He was just climbing into bed in nothing but his boxers when he heard the dreaded sound. What now? He really needed his phone. What was the worst that could happen? He put his pillow over his head and tuned out the buzzer's second buzz. He already knew what was the worst, didn't he?

If he opened that door, her sparkling smile would melt him. Her sensual voice would entice and he would be helpless to resist. They would start dating and their demise would be imminent. He thought all of this as he unbolted the door and opened it just a crack.

"Hello," he said as brown eyes met green. He was surprised to see that she wasn't alone. She was with a man he had never seen before.

"Hi. John? I found your phone. You dropped it at the store today. My name is Stacy and this is my dad, Jack Stark." John looked at the man, suspiciously.

"Uh, thanks. I'm not really dressed for company." John said quickly, taking the phone.

"That's okay. Bye, now," Stacy said, giving him a sweet smile and turned away. Then she suddenly remembered something and turned back. "Oh, by the way, I added a song to your music. It's from my brother's band. It's called 'Utter Devastation'. Listen to it if you get a chance." She winked at him and walked away.

The Killer 10

Bradley Darewood

Mike stirred the chicken in the skillet. It had been decomposing in the refrigerator for over a week but if he just cooked it long enough it should kill all of the bacteria. Right?

"Do I look fat?" Mike mused to his roommate, pinching his abs self-consciously.

Joe looked at his friend flatly. "Do you even own a penis?"

"I'm seeing Alicia--"

"Tomorrow."

"Wait, how did you--"

"I hear all your phone conversations."

"That's creepy, dude."

"Trust me, if I could get a lobotomy to make the voices stop, I would. You're on the phone in the fucking living room. And the kitchen. And in the goddamn bathroom."

"She likes to talk--"

"Six times a day." Joe pitched his voice in his best whiny falsetto, "Oh baby, you're too beautiful for that job. Fuck the office work. They're lucky to have you."

"You wouldn't understand. Long distance relationships are hard."

"She's cheating on you."

"What?"

"I said she's cheating on you."

"You haven't even met her."

"High-maintenance girls always cheat. They're never satisfied. It's like a psychological defense so they can tell themselves you deserved to be cheated on when they're boning some jackass they met at the grocery store."

"I'm not taking relationship advice from a loser with no girlfriend."

"Trust me, I'd be single till the end of time if it meant I never had to be in a relationship with your girlfriend. I'm traumatized just overhearing it on the phone."

"Luckily, I could give a shit about your opinion. In fifteen minutes, I'm going to be on the road and on the way to see my boo."

"Your *boo*?" Joe made a face at the word. "Wait-- in fifteen minutes? It's almost 10 PM, and it's an eight-hour drive to LA."

Mike slid the chicken off of the skillet and onto his plate. "This is the only three-day weekend I've had since I moved here, and she wants me there right away." He shoveled a forkful of chicken into his mouth.

"Jesus," Joe rolled his eyes as he walked out of the kitchen in disgust. "You're not taking the 10 freeway, are you?" he called from the living room.

"What do you mean?" Mike followed his roommate in curiosity, plate in hand. "Of course I'm taking the 10. The 8 takes two hours longer."

"Jesus. At night? Aren't you afraid of the Killer 10?"

"The what?"

Joe looked at his friend incredulously. "The serial killer. Do you live in a cave?"

"That sounds like a swimsuit calendar, not the name for a serial killer." Mike took another bite of chicken.

"There's twelve months in a calendar not ten, dipshit. He's named 'the Killer 10' after the freeway. The I-10."

"That's a lot of ground for a serial killer to cover."

"At rest stops, gas stations, anywhere dark and

secluded off of the 10, he bludgeons his victims to death, cuts out their tongue, then cuts their ears off and puts them in their mouth."

"Why?"

"Fuck if I know, he's a serial killer. Don't ask why. He's crazy. When he's done, he scrawls a number in his victim's blood, on a building or asphalt or wherever."

"A number?"

"A tally. The last one was number eleven."

"I was thinking he'd stop at ten...."

"This is serious, Mike. I'm urging you as a friend. Take the 8."

"I like to think of you less as a friend and more like a jackass I live with who has no idea what he's talking about. If this serial killer you invented was real, I would have seen something on the news."

Joe guffawed. "Who the hell watches the news anymore? Everyone's talking about it on Facebook."

Mike raised an eyebrow. "Betty White's funeral has been trending on Facebook more times than I can count. The first time I believed it and almost cried."

Joe winced. "Betty *White?* You really *don't* own a penis."

"I'm not making a decision based upon 'news' you got from status updates sandwiched between cat memes." Mike stuffed the last bit of chicken into his mouth and set his plate on the living room coffee table. It really didn't taste rotten at all with enough ketchup. He grabbed his duffel bag off the couch.

"You're just going to leave that there?" Joe said, motioning at the plate.

"I'll wash it when I get back."

"In three days?"

Mike smiled at his roommate's irritation as he let himself out the door.

His hair stood on end as the night's chill ran its

invisible fingers over his skin. The streetlight outside their house had long been broken, as was the light inside his car. Darkness was as thick as soup, the moon hidden behind clouds crisscrossed by the gnarled silhouettes of dead trees. Shadows upon shadows gave the street an eerie depth.

A low grumble faintly registered in Mike's ears, but he paid it no mind. Popping the back door of his car open, he tossed his bag in without a second thought. He shuddered. He would definitely need to use the heater tonight.

The roads were empty as he found his way to the 10 freeway. Not a soul in sight. Even for late at night, the freeway was oddly empty. Maybe Joe *had* been telling the truth and there really was a serial killer. Mike shrugged. Less traffic wasn't a bad thing.

It wasn't long before Mike found himself missing the traffic. He was driving alone. For hours. Nothing but black existed beyond the halo of his headlights. Empty monotonous darkness. Mike shook his head, catching himself-- had he just blacked out? He was still in his lane at least. This was going to be a long drive. A low grumble whispered in his ears once again. If he was going to survive this ride, he was *really* going to need some coffee. The lights of Phoenix appeared in the distance. Had he already driven two hours?

Phoenix. What a shithole. Did he really want coffee from *Phoenix*? A gas station French Vanilla cappuccino would probably mean oily dregs in heated vats that got cleaned once a year, refilled by a crusty old woman who didn't wash her hands. Mike cringed. *Phoenix.*

His eyes rolled into the back of his head once again; this time he nearly swerved off the road. He was going to need coffee *fast*. The grumble returned, slightly louder than before.

Mike made his way to the nearest exit. A stretch and

coffee. That was exactly what he needed.

His headlights revealed concrete, dirt and chain-link fences-- the lifeless Phoenix landscape Mike reviled. Where the hell was a gas station?

The grumble was getting louder. Mike's eyes lit up in alarm. That noise had come from his stomach. *Oh god. The chicken!*

Coffee faded from his mind as the all-consuming urge to shit took over.

Fuck! Where the fuck is a gas station! He cursed himself for cooking rotten meat. He was such an idiot! *Oh god, it hurts.*

A gas station appeared on the left side of the street, on the other side of a median. *Damn!* With a rapid jerk of the wheel, he whipped across the road, grinding the bottom of his car with a loud scrape in the process.

Accelerator to the floor, he tore into the gas station and screeched to a halt beside the entrance to the QwikieMart. Leaping out of his car, he rushed to the doors. With a loud bang, they resisted his attempt to pull them open. He tried again. The doors were locked shut.

Peering inside, past the candy bars and coffee, he could see the restroom sign, teasing him with the false promise of release. To the right was a counter with a woman behind it, looking extremely displeased. She rolled her eyes motioning to the window.

Mike hobbled over, using every ounce of his will to clench his anus. He put his face to the steel mesh hole in the bulletproof glass. "Thank god you're here, I really need to--"

"Just a minute," she held up her left hand as her right hand finished a text message on her phone. "Okay, go ahead."

"I just really need to use the restroom. I think I'm going to die."

She looked at him flatly, as if disgusted he had the

audacity to ask to use the toilet. "M-mn."

"M-mn?" Mike asked in confusion.

"No."

"Please, I'm begging you."

"Beg away. The restrooms are closed to the public."

"There's a sign, I can see it from right here."

"There's another sign on the bathroom door. It says 'CLOSED'."

"Please, I'll buy something… or I can just give you some money or something."

"Are you trying to *bribe* me, asshole? Who do I look like to you? I ain't opening that door for *no one*."

"I swear I'm not a robber. I'm not a serial killer. I just really need to shit."

"We don't let people use the toilets when there *isn't* a serial killer on the lose. No. Public. Restrooms." The woman pulled a firearm out from under the counter.

"Jesus!" Mike begged, "Please! I'll do anything you want, just let me use the toilet."

The woman hefted her gun. "Get out of here before I call the police."

Phoenix. Police state of paranoid assholes with guns. The city made the national news on a regular basis for abuses committed by its police.

Mike wobbled to his car, his stomach feeling like it might explode. How was he going to bend? "Jesus, I hate this city," he murmured.

Peeling off as fast as he could go, Mike found his way back to the freeway. He pressed his left foot against the floor of the car as hard as it would go, his face contorted in an agonized wince. He clutched his seat belt in his mouth, biting it and screaming at the same time. His stomach grumbled again, like a volcano threatening to explode.

With a violent turn of the steering wheel, he pulled off into the next exit. He barely remembered pulling into the gas station and parking; the agony in his stomach obliterated all other thought.

"I... I need to use the restroom," he gasped into the bulletproof window.

"I'm really sorry," the man on the other side said. "We don't have a public restroom here."

"For fuck's sake, is there any public restroom in all of Phoenix?"

"The police told us not to let people in the bathrooms. Too many drug addicts. And terrorists."

"You're worried that a terrorist is going to take a shit. In Phoenix. Why the fuck would a *terrorist* come to Ari-fucking-zona to take a shit?"

"I don't know. Terrorists is crazy. You never know where they want to shit."

Mike closed his eyes and put his hand over his face in agonized frustration.

"Look," the attendant continued, "there's a Mexican restaurant across the street that's open late. They've got a restroom if you buy some tacos."

Mike didn't even wait to say thanks. In a strange combination of a wobble and a sprint, he rushed in the direction of the Mexican restaurant. He couldn't risk trying to sit in the car again. If he bent like that, he'd soil himself for sure.

As he approached the restaurant, his heart began to sink. The place was completely empty. It had to be closed. He shook the locked door with all his strength, tears rolling from his eyes. "Please! For the love of god!" he shouted to no one in particular.

His body couldn't take any more. There was no way this was going to end well. He didn't think he could even make it to his car. Mike wobble-sprinted his way to the back of the restaurant.

His stomach grumbled again, Mother Nature's guttural call.

Jesusfuck! Oh god, Jesusfuck! Is that a new word? If it's not, it should be. I think I invented a new word. Mike made a mental note to look up "Jesusfuck" in the urban dictionary when he got to Alicia's house.

Thoughts of the urban dictionary vanished as the deadly storm brewing in his stomach churned once again. It was coming. It was coming now.

Mike ripped the shoe off of his right foot and pulled his right leg up through his pants and underpants. The bundle hung wrapped around his left leg as Mike dropped into a squat.

In a moment it was over. His clothes gripped in one hand, his other hand gripping his hair, he hovered over a pile of shit as his bladder emptied itself. He moaned, then panted in relief. He could feel the urine seeping into his right sock, but he didn't care. "Thank god," he whispered to himself.

A disturbing thought interrupted his moment of Zen. How was he going to wipe? Looking around, Mike saw nothing but concrete and dirt. "Fuck."

Easing the clothes off of his leg, he eyed the bundle sadly. He was going to have to sacrifice his favorite pair of underwear. The pair he always wore to impress Alicia.

With a determined face he wadded up his underwear and began to clean himself. "Fuck you, Phoenix," Mike murmured.

Suddenly, he froze in mid-wipe.

A shadow moved.

Mike's mind filled with horrific thoughts of being bludgeoned to death pants-less and in his own feces. Something crept closer, the sound of its wheezing breath loud, deep and unnerving.

He looked around frantically for something to defend himself with. He had nothing but his soiled underpants. The dark figure approached.

An unkempt man with a ratty beard and crazed eyes crept out of the darkness. The man's chest heaved rapidly as he breathed at a breakneck pace. He reached into his oversized coat. Mike whimpered. He cringed, turning his face away.

"S-sorry. I-I just… I had a napkin."

Mike opened his eyes. The stranger was gripping his frizzy, unwashed hair with one hand, while offering a napkin with the other. He motioned to Mike's underwear, brown with his own feces.

"Uh, thanks, I think I got it handled."

"S-sorry. I-I didn't mean to scare you." The homeless man backed away, retreating like a beaten dog, embarrassed that he'd interrupted Mike's shit.

"No, it's okay. That army jacket. Are you a vet?"

The man didn't say anything. He clutched his jacket till his hands went white.

"Why… why are you out here?" Mike continued.

"I've seen… things. The things I've seen. Horrible. Horrible things."

"In the war?"

"No."

"Where then?"

"Not… not in the war."

Mike shrugged; he wasn't going to get an answer. Clearly, the man was traumatized. He looked down. Perhaps it was his exposed genitals that had made the homeless guy uncomfortable. Mike slid his pants back on and dug into his pocket. All he had was a twenty. "Fuck it. Here." He held out the bill.

"I didn't ask for your money."

"Take it. Buy a forty. Wipe your ass with it. I don't care. Let's just say I have a new appreciation for what it's like to be stuck out here surrounded by assholes with no place to shit. At least I get to drive my way out of here. You're stuck."

The homeless man reached his hand out and took the bill, looking away shyly. He held it close, gingerly, like a girl who had just been given a stuffed bear and a box of chocolates for Valentine's Day.

"Look, I know that's pretty much nothing. But I'm sorry. I'm sorry for what happened to you. For whatever it was that you saw."

A darkness touched the homeless man's eyes. "I'll see it again."

"I don't underst--"

"Nhuh."

"What?"

"NHUH!" Spittle spewed out of the indigent's mouth. Thick snot dripped from his nose. "NHUUUUH!" His eyes rolled back into his head.

Mike jumped back involuntarily.

"I see it! I can see it! There are no birds. Just me. Tweet! Tweet-tweet!"

"Holy fuck, you're scaring the shit out of me."

"You're not scared yet. Not yet." The man picked at his hair, like a tweaker with a nervous twitch. "I see it. I see it before it happens. I see it all." He slapped his hand against this head, as if trying to bang the images out of his ears.

"Are you... having a seizure?" Mike took another step back, unsure of what to do.

"Jesusfuck!" the homeless man shouted.

Jesusfuck? I must have said it out loud. He must have heard me say Jesusfuck. Mike wrung his hands.

"Jesusfuck! Three times! Jesusfuck!"

Mike opened his mouth to say something, but his thoughts seemed caught in his mouth.

"The first time, pain. The second time, fear! Jesusfuck! JESUSFUCK! The third time!" The homeless man punched his temple, thick white globs hanging from his nose, froth dripping out the side of his mouth.

"And… the third time?" Mike asked, unable to resist.
"The third time! The third time! The third time!"
"Uh…"
"The third time… *dread.*"

The homeless man stood silent for a moment. Mike watched, unable to move.

The man gripped his hair tight in his hand, and looked Mike straight in the face with those eyes rolled back in his head. "Tweet-tweet! Tweet-tweet! I am not a bird. I AM NOT A BIRD!!!" he shrieked.

Suddenly he stiffened, then crumpled to his knees like a lifeless doll. He knelt there for a moment, his head hung low, breathing.

"Th… thank you for the twenty," he said softly.
"I, uh…. You're welcome. I gotta… uh, go."
"Just… try to get back to Alicia. Try."

Mike's blood ran cold. *How did he know her name?* Mike must have mentioned her and just forgot. He *must* have.

Mike made his way back to his car. He hadn't found coffee, but his adrenaline was pumping.

Speeding on the freeway, he was relieved to see the lights of Phoenix disappear behind him. That had to be the creepiest homeless man he'd ever met in his life. That was actually the only homeless man Mike had ever met, but he felt confident that, had he met any others, they would have been less creepy.

A blue sign appeared in the darkness.

"ENTERING DESERT. NO SERVICES FOR 60 MILES."

They need a sign like that when entering Phoenix, Mike mused.

He attempted to take his mind off of Phoenix and the creepy homeless man by turning on the radio. The harsh sound of static filled his car. He pushed a button and the radio searched for signal, cycling thorough numbers until it landed, at last, on a working station.

Christian rock. Mike winced. At least it wasn't country music. Actually, it was kind of catchy. "Keep on, keep on. You're not alone!" He sang along in the car. Until the music stopped and the radio announcer, a woman with a thick twang, came on.

"Now that's such a nice song about turnin' the other cheek, but when Jesus said all that, it was in a time before there was terrorists. I can guarantee that if Jesus were born again today, he'd be a proud member of the NRA. Let me--"

Mike turned off the radio, wincing once again. He had a headache. He had forgotten why he always kept the radio off on these trips. There was no quicker way to remind himself why he was an atheist than to listen to Christian radio.

The quiet of the drive was interrupted by a low grumble. *Oh no.*

His eyes scanned desperately for some sign of an exit.

"REST AREA, 25 MILES"

Thank god. A rest stop. No gas station attendants with guns. Just toilets.

Mike pushed the accelerator as far down as it would go. He couldn't spare any more underwear to use as toilet paper-- if he even made it out of the car. He could feel his insides tremble as his stomach rumbled once again. He had to make it to that rest stop!

The world exploded in agony, and he clenched his jaw in strain. Could he burst a blood vessel this way? His eyes scanned the side of the road for another sign.

"REST AREA, 15 MILES"

Fifteen miles? He'd only driven ten miles! It felt like an hour had passed! *What the fuck!* Mike gripped the steering wheel so hard he feared it might break, and shrieked into the air.

"Count. I need to count," he told himself. "Like counting sheep. I'll count the seconds of each minute until I get there."

Fifteen miles, fifteen minutes. Well, at this speed, more like ten minutes.

"One. Two. THREE!" Mike shouted as every muscle in his body clenched, trying to hold the diseased chicken in his intestines. "F-f-foooooouuuuurrrr! OH GOD!" Mike's face twisted until the road blurred, but the car stayed in its lane. "Five! Five-Five-FIVE!" He punched the dashboard in an attempt to distract himself from his pain. He rocked back and forth in his seat. *How many seconds are there in ten minutes?* "Six! Seven! Oh fuck, SEVEN!" *Six hundred. Fuck. Me. SIX HUNDRED.* "Eight! Motherfucking eight!"

The empty road stared impassively back at him. Mike screamed the numbers, calling upon every reserve of strength he had. "What? You want a piece of me, you piece of shit freeway? Nine! That's right! Nine!" Sweat dripped down Mike's flushed face. If he bit his lip any harder, he'd draw blood.

"Ten." *The Killer 10.*

"Eleven." *Eleven victims.*

"FUCK COUNTING!" Mike punched the dashboard again, with a cry of rage. "*For the love of god let me exit!*"

"REST AREA, 5 MILES"

How had that happened? The counting worked! He was almost there.

Five more miles. Five more miles. He could do this. Four! Four more miles!

Mike's tears of pain turned to tears of joy. He might not shit his pants after all!

"EXIT 60, REST AREA"

Euphoria sunk into Mike's very bones as he sped his car down the exit ramp to the unlit rest area. He parked his car between a Jetta and a beat-up old truck. The only cars he'd seen all night. He didn't pay them much mind-- he was focused on one thing and one thing only: the toilet.

Mike felt like an athlete finishing a marathon. *Fuck runners. My sphincter could probably compete in the Olympics after all this.* He sprinted to his finish line: the Men's Room. Swinging the door open, he was met with impenetrable blackness and the smell of piss and shit. Mike stumbled through the darkness as fast as he could wobble. *Of course the lights* would *be out. Just my luck.*

Heet. Heet. Heet. Heet. It sounded like some sort of strange, nasal birdcall. A bird must be trapped in the bathroom.

A loud grumble shook his stomach once again. There was no time to grab his phone. He had to find the toilet *now.*

Heet. Heet. Heet. Heet.

Mike felt his way to the nearest stall, tearing the door open and reaching for the wall. He grabbed a support bar. Good. He was in the handicapped bathroom. Those were his favorite toilets. They were the most spacious.

"Ew." Mike winced. The floor was wet and sticky.

He didn't have the luxury of hesitating. Forcing his pants down, he threw his ass in the direction of the toilet just in time to launch a burning stream of high-velocity shit into the toilet bowl. *Gross.* The toilet seat was sticky and wet too. And it was *warm.* The piss must be fresh. Mike shuddered.

Heet. Heet. Heet. Heet. What a weird sounding bird. It was so close. Maybe even in the stall with him.

His bowels released, Mike sighed in relief. He reached into his pocket for his phone. He would need a light to find the toilet paper. He flicked the light on.

A face! Inches to his right was a girl crouched over something. Her face was red with a coat of fresh, glistening blood. A bloody finger to her lips. "Shh!"

Mike let out a high-pitched shriek and leapt off the toilet, his dick flopping in the chilly air. His phone tumbled to the ground with an unpleasant crack. "Jesusfuck!"

His pants still at his ankles, he dropped to the ground. The sticky wet ground. Slick. Slick with... blood. *Like the toilet.* He had been sitting on *blood.* He had seen something behind the girl, on the wall of the stall... *Oh god.* It had been a number... Twelve, scrawled in blood. *Oh. God.*

Heet. Heet. Heet. Heet.

Shaking, his hands and knees wet with blood, he felt along the floor for his phone. He felt... something slimy. A slug? He reached next to it and found his phone. The screen felt cracked. *Fuck.* He pushed the button on the side of the phone, and a spider web of shattered glass lit up. That hadn't been a slug. In the puddle of blood before him was a severed tongue.

Heet. Heet. Heet. Heet.

Mike's eyes lifted slowly. A girl, drenched in blood crouched over a man.

Heet. Heet. Heet. Heet.

His face... what was left of his face, was unrecognizable. Blood oozed from the side of his torn mouth, his teeth scattered around him. His nose... where was his nose? Bashed in, perhaps. His jaw hung, dislocated, twisted into an unnatural shape. His ears had been cut off and stuffed into his mouth.

Heet. Heet. Heet. Heet.

The man's chest heaved up and down, hyperventilating, his mangled, tongue-less face making the only sound it could: *Heet. Heet. Heet. Heet.*

That was *not* a bird.

"Holy fuck," Mike breathed.

The girl pointed at his phone in alarm.

"I'm not getting any reception out here. Besides, I think it's broken."

"No," the girl hissed in an alarmed whisper, "turn it off! He'll see!" She pointed at his exposed manhood. "And for Christ's sake pull your pants up."

"Who's 'he'?" Mike pulled his trousers up, slipping his phone into his pocket.

"*Him,*" her voice trembled. "Oh god, he's going to kill us all."

Heet. Heet. Heet. Heet.

"Please tell me you have a gun," she whispered in desperation. "We have to kill him."

"No, I don't."

"You're kidding."

"I'm not from Arizona."

Heet. Heet. Heet. Heet.

Suddenly he felt a bloody hand over his mouth. "He's coming," he heard her whisper in his ear. He could taste the blood on her hand, feel the blood from the toilet sticking to the back of his legs. His heart pounded like a drum about to explode.

The door to the restroom creaked open, and the sound of sluggish footsteps filled the room. There was the clank of something metal. Something metal in his hand.

Heet. Heet. Heet. Heet.

The footsteps approached, then stopped just in front of the stall door.

Heet. Heet. Heet. Heet.

The locked stall creaked as the killer leaned softly against it. A ragged breath escaped his lips. Something in his hands was dripping… with blood?

What the hell is he doing? Mike wondered. He wanted to stand, but his legs were shaking. The girl's hand was over his mouth, but Mike didn't dare breathe.

Heet. Heet. Heet. Heet.

On the other side of the door, the killer's breath

seemed to catch, and an agonized moan escaped his lips. Shuddered, rapid breaths escaped the killer's heaving lungs. Was he... crying? Sadness turned to rage, and the killer let out a shriek. Something metal struck the wall. Debris rained on the sticky bathroom floor.

Mike jumped involuntarily. His lungs ached from holding his breath.

Heet. Heet. Heet. Heet.

The moaning whimper returned, but the killer turned away from the door. He slowly shuffled out of the bathroom.

Mike released his breath, then immediately inhaled, his lungs thirsty for air. "Holy shit," he gasped. If he hadn't just used the toilet, he would without question want to piss himself in fear. "We just... we just need to get to my car. We'll get out of here without him seeing us."

"Your car won't start."

"How do you know?"

"Because that's the first thing he does. He cuts the wires to your car. That's what he did to me. What he did to... him."

Heet. Heet. Heet. Heet.

"We're fucked. Oh god, we're *fucked*." Mike gripped his hair with his hands.

"I have a baseball bat. In my car."

"And... how is that going to start my car?"

Heet. Heet. Heet. Heet.

"You have to kill him. You have to take the bat and kill him."

"I can't! I don't even know how to play baseball! I do... back squats... and bench press.... These muscles are just for show!"

Thwack! The girl slapped Mike across the face. She had a solid slap for a girl that size. Her hand left a sticky trail, the other man's blood smeared across his face. "Pull it together. If you don't, we are *both* going to die!"

Heet. Heet. Heet. Heet.

"Okay," Mike took a deep breath.

"Are you ready?"

"No."

Heet. Heet. Heet. Heet.

"Do you want to end up like him?" He couldn't see her, but he knew she was motioning to the mangled man on the stall floor.

Mike didn't think he could do this, but it was now or never. He stood, his legs shaking uncontrollably. He opened the stall door and felt his way across the dark bathroom. The girl followed, gripping his left hand tightly.

Heet. Heet. Heet. Heet.

He found the restroom door. Gently pressing it forward, he peeked through the crack. He could see the killer, seven hundred feet away. The murderer stood facing the beat-up truck, its hood popped. His head was shaved, and his bloodstained wife-beater revealed the rippling muscles of his back. He stood a hulking six-foot-two. In his hand was a giant monkey wrench, perhaps a foot long, red with fresh blood.

"How are we going to get to the car? He's right there!" Mike hissed.

"We can get closer, hide by the vending machines. When he moves away from the cars, we make a run for my trunk." She pressed her keys in his hand.

Mike's heart was in his throat as he left the bathrooms. He hadn't been on a treadmill in ages. *Oh god, we're going to die.*

The killer seemed absorbed with the truck, tinkering around under the hood as Mike and the girl slid carefully out of the Men's Room. A second building would provide shelter, if they could get to it. Mike crept forward on his shaking legs, trying to quell the panic inside. Soon, they were hidden from view once again. Sliding around the back of the second building brought them to the vending machines. Their low hum grew louder as Mike and his companion approached them. He looked at the girl, her face glowing in the neon light of the machines. He could feel them vibrate as he pressed against them, peeking around ever so slowly. The killer was right there, less than 30 feet away.

The muscle-bound behemoth set his blood-coated wrench on the ground as he reached into the hood.

The girl nudged Mike, mouthing the word "now."

Mike shook his head in horror.

The girl nudged again.

The muscular man pulled himself out from under the hood. Whatever opportunity had been was lost. Wiping his hands on his pants, the man walked to the back of the truck.

The girl shoved Mike forward.

Mike could barely hear the sound of the killer rummaging through the back of his truck over the pounding of his heart. After what seemed like an eternity, they were crouched on the far side of the girl's car. She motioned toward the trunk. But Mike's eyes were in the opposite direction. The bloody wrench lay unattended on the sidewalk at the front of the nearby truck.

Before he could stop himself, Mike leapt forward.

The killer froze, perking his ears, then raced to the front of the truck. The hulking shadow approached, but with a cry Mike dove onto the ground. He grabbed the wrench, his body scraping against concrete.

The killer lifted his arm to strike, but Mike swept the wrench with all his strength, snapping the killer's forearm with a loud crack. The bald man howled in agony, clutching his arm. Mike took a second swipe to the man's face, teeth spraying onto the ground.

Blood flowed from the man's broken lips. "Ghuh-hu-huh..." he moaned.

He didn't... he didn't have a *tongue*. Was that why he cut his victims' tongues out? Because he didn't have a tongue of his own? Mike winced at the hideous monster before him. A hulking mute creature, driven to madness. The savage monstrosity fell to his knees, a defeated look on his face. Like he wanted to die.

"Kill him!" the girl shrieked from behind him.

"He's not... he's not fighting!"

"Quick! Before he changes his mind!"

Mike swung the wrench into the man's face, and it hit with a sickening crunch. Mike did it again and again, as hard and fast as he could. Bone cracked and blood splattered as Mike demolished the man's face. The killer fell to the ground, but Mike didn't stop, shrieking as he bludgeoned his victim to death.

Chest heaving for breath, Mike looked at his handiwork in disgust. What was left of the man's face was unrecognizable. Blood oozed from the side of his torn mouth, his teeth scattered around him. His nose... where was his nose? Bashed in, perhaps. His jaw hung, dislocated, twisted into an unnatural shape. But the man was still alive, in agony, breathing rapidly.

Heet. Heet. Heet. Heet.

The girl pushed past Mike and knelt over the killer.

"I wouldn't--"

She pulled a pocketknife out of her pocket, and began to saw off the man's ears.

"What... what are you doing?"

Ignoring Mike, she stuffed the ears in the man's motionless mouth. "It never takes much," she said casually. She plunged the knife into his midsection, cutting enough of a space to reach her hand in, soaking it with blood. "When men are afraid, violence always follows." On the sidewalk beside the man, she scrawled the number thirteen with the dead man's innards.

Jesusfuck.

"You're... the Killer 10," Mike said, backing away in horror. The bloody wrench fell to the ground with a clatter.

"No." The girl offered a wicked smile. "You are."

Cake & Quill

Biographies

Our editor

Catherine Lenderi

Catherine Lenderi has been working as an English teacher since 1998 and has frequently been employed as a freelance editor / proofreader. She works with authors of various genres. In the "Books" section of her website, you can see some of the books she has recently worked on and the authors' testimonies regarding her services.
http://catsedits.weebly.com/

Our writers (in order of appearance in this book)

S.A. Shields

S.A. Shields is a twenty something mother of three boys, who spends too much time writing and drinking coffee. Her debut novel, Don't Speak, is a mature young adult fiction, which tackles those dark teenage issues no one wants to speak about.
http://writersspill.weebly.com/

Chloe Hammond

Born in Liverpool in 1975, she grew up in West Wales. She studied Behavioural Sciences at the University of Glamorgan, but pestered her lecturers to allow her some modules of Creative Writing.

She always planned to write – life just got in the way. Married, she now lives by the sea, just outside Cardiff, with two bonkers dogs and a suitably lazy cat. Diagnosed with anxiety and depression, she finally made time to write, finding writing a stimulation to help her through every crisis. She wrote The Price Of Love when her husband had a heart attack. She chose the title from an article which said that grief is the price of love.
http://www.chloehammond-author.weebly.com/

J.R. Biery

J.R. Biery is a retired teacher who loves to write. Sold numerous fiction and nonfiction pieces to magazines while a stay-at home mom. Had one novel, Potter's Field, accepted and published by Advance Books, a small press no longer in business. Now has seventeen works up on Amazon, twelve are novels.
http://www.jrbiery.wordpress.com

Charlotte Stirling

Charlotte Stirling divides her time between Germany and Scotland with her husband, two children and a depressed Beagle. Her flash fiction has been published in Literary Orphans, Camroc Press Review and Spelk Fiction. When she isn't writing or baking cupcakes, she is thinking about writing, reading, designing book covers, gaming or watching dark, blood-splattered dramas like the Walking Dead, Ray Donavon and Sons of Anarchy.
http://tabby007.tumblr.com/
http://tabathadesign.tumblr.com/

James Warren McAllister

James Warren McAllister is a Registered Respiratory Therapist living in Central New York State. James has been interested in science fiction since a friend in Junior High School lent him the Lensmen Series of books by E. E. "Doc" Smith. This interest was further spiked by Star Trek and then Star Wars.
http://fortiterpublishing.com

William Douglas Frank

From his humble beginnings in a Texas township, William Douglas Frank has reached a level of literary genius that challenges God himself. Small town preachers quake in their boots when he approaches and children wet themselves in fear. The dread that he shall unleash upon you in this anthology is but a tiny glimpse of his horrific literary power, muted only by his mercy, to protect your virgin eyes from permanent scarring.
http://frankthetank881.wix.com/wdfrank

Tina Rath

Tina lives in London with her husband and some cats. She has had around 60 short stories published, and has several novels, including a fantasy trilogy on the stocks. She has a PhD in *The Vampire in Popular Fiction,* she's an actress – recent jobs include Hideous Creature and Professional Yawner. Plus she's a story-teller as well as a writer and a Queen Victoria Lookalike.
www.christinarath.wordpress.com

Rubianne Wood

Rubianne Wood is a writer of paranormal mysteries. She's from Southeast Kansas where she grew up in a small town and currently lives there happily with her family. She is the mother of three boisterous teenagers, two dogs, and a cat. Though her home-life can be pretty chaotic, she was born with the God-given talent to block out the noise and live in her own world for hours at a time in order to write.
http://rubianneparanormalmysteries.com

Angelika Rust

Angelika Rust was born in Vienna in 1977. These days, she lives in Germany, with her husband, two children, a despotic couple of cats and a hyperactive dog. After having tried almost every possible job from pizza delivery girl to HR consultant, she now makes a living knowing a little English.
http://angelikarust.wordpress.com/

Russell Cruse

Russell Cruse lives in a beautiful village in rural England with a long-suffering wife, two dogs and a cat. It wasn't always the case. Some have said that his stories bear witness to a lifetime of bitterness, regret and depredation but those people are idiots; his stories are only stories – as all stories are.
http://www.russellcruse.com

T.M. Hogan

T.M. Hogan is a Greek Australian mum of three, who refuses to grow up. Grade-A crazy that makes life explode with colour and noise. A blooming dark fantasy writer, Walking Through Darkness is her first story to be published, with a trilogy titled Ganymede in the works.
https://www.facebook.com/T-M-Hogan-490418697803077

J. Cassidy

J. Cassidy used to be an oak tree growing in a park in England. He still likes to be decorated once a year. Pink, sparkly fluffles and rainbows make everything better.
https://6twistedbiscuits.wordpress.com

Donald B. Stephens

There was once a man who lived in a boot. He tried writing books and found it a hoot. They asked him for a short story, and he quickly complied. But when asked for a bio, they said he had lied.
http://donaldbstephens.com

Tom Greenwood

Born and lived in Scotland all his life apart for a year down in Sheffield. Married with two daughters. Trying to learn Spanish. Wrote a book. Likes beer. Does computers for a living and gets frustrated at all the nonsense that goes on in a (fairly) big company. Err nothing really exciting. Never won a nobel prize, though

he once did win a bottle of rum.
http://www.aslightmistakeinthecode.com

Adam Oster

Adam Oster writes tales of adventure where he can pretend he's gone on wild excursions across time and space all for the purposes of coming up with an entertaining story. He also likes pizza.
http://www.fatmogul.com/

Bradley Darewood

Born just before Halloween, Bradley Darewood has a special love of the macabre. He writes everything from psychotic sorceresses to indigents in space, but his contribution here involves a metrosexual man's encounter with a serial killer on the freeway. Keep an eye out for his in-progress fantasy novel Unsung Heroes.
http://www.nerdempire.org

Content

Can You See Me..1

The Price of Love..21

Vicious People..23

Boo..29

The Last One..31

Whispers Of Lavender......................................35

The Place of the Lost..37

Trapped...45

The Wrong Girl..49

Mr Bark...59

Phantom Dollhouse..61

Night Bus...63

Flight...79

Walking Through Darkness...............................85

Wrath Of A Limbless God...............................109

Never Again...111

A Storm Blows Through Polecat County........119

We're not in Kansas...127

Cryo...129

The Agony of Defeat..135

Sea Of Contradictions..137

Hippopotomonstrosesquipedaliophobia......................139

Late..155

The Beginning of the End...159

The Killer 10..167

Biographies..189

Printed in Great Britain
by Amazon